LADY GOLD INVESTIGATES ~ VOLUME 3

COMPANION SHORT STORIES TO GINGER GOLD MYSTERIES

LEE STRAUSS
NORM STRAUSS

la plume
PRESS

Library and Archives Canada Cataloguing in Publication Title: Lady Gold
investigates : a short read cozy historical 1920s mystery collection / Lee Strauss.
Names: Strauss, Lee (Novelist), author. Description: Short stories. | Contents: v. 3.
The case of missing time -- The case of the unlucky cricketeer. Identifiers: Canadiana
(print) 20190131608 | Canadiana (ebook) 20190131624 | ISBN 9781774090718 (v. 3 :
hardcover) | ISBN 9781774090701 (v. 3 : softcover) | ISBN 9781774090725 (v. 3 :
IngramSpark softcover) | ISBN 9781774090640 (v. 3 : Kindle) | ISBN 9781774090695
(v. 3 : EPUB) Classification: LCC PS8637.T739 L34 2019 | DDC C813/.6—dc23

THE CASE OF THE
MISSING TIME

1

—————

$\mathcal{I}$t wasn't often that someone came through the front door of *Lady Gold Investigations* totally unannounced. Clients either rung up by telephone first or had a message delivered in order to make an appointment. So, when the door suddenly swung open on a rainy Thursday afternoon, making the doorbell chime, Mrs. Ginger Reed, her Boston terrier, Boss, and her sister-in-law, Felicia Gold, who worked as Ginger's assistant, all looked up in surprise.

A slim gentleman in his thirties stood in the office door, looking confused. Hatless, he wore a rumpled three-piece tweed suit with a white shirt and a loosely tied red tie. Though it was raining heavily outside, he didn't carry an umbrella, and his dark-blond hair was dripping wet. He had no moustache or beard, though the shadow on his jaw proved he hadn't shaved for a while. Ginger thought he could well be called handsome, and his long, angular face looked rather familiar though she couldn't quite place him. At the moment, his blue eyes conveyed bewilderment as though he had just woken up in a strange room. He looked at Felicia and then at Ginger.

"Can we help you?" Felicia asked.

"I do apologise." He lingered near the entrance, blinking rapidly. Though his suit was bedraggled, on closer inspection

Ginger noted it was of good quality and his two-tone brown and white Oxford wing-tipped shoes looked new and costly.

Ginger pushed a lock of red hair behind her ears, brushing against her ruby and diamond earring, and glanced down at Boss. Her beloved dog was an excellent judge of character and could immediately sense if there was danger. It brought Ginger a measure of comfort when Boss relaxed on his belly, his black and white head cocked quizzically to one side.

Ginger stood, smoothed the pleated fern-green skirt of her two-piece crepe de Chine frock, and motioned towards the leather chairs that faced her large wooden desk. "Do come in and have a seat," Ginger said. "It is certainly a wet day today and you must be chilled."

Ginger had recently taken over the lease of a shop that had formerly held a cobbler's shop and was proud of how the renovations had turned the premises into an efficient and comfortable office from which to conduct her investigations.

"Yes, of course. Thank you." As the man moved towards the seat, he displayed a definite limp, favouring his right foot. "I am sorry about the water." He looked down at his wet shoes. Felicia fetched a clean towel from the cupboard in the corridor. "Oh, very kind," he said, accepting the offering, then proceeding to dry his face and hair.

"I'm Mrs. Ginger Reed, and this is my assistant, Miss Gold. Now, what brings you into our office today?"

"I'm very pleased to meet you both."

In spite of the polite phrase, the man appeared agitated and uneasy. Ginger smiled warmly, hoping to soothe him. "And might we know your name?" she asked.

"Well, here's the thing, madam. I was just walking down this street... and I..." The man faltered. "Well, I saw your sign on the door." He looked at them both as if waiting for them to finish the sentence. Ginger glanced at Felicia before saying, "Go on."

"Well I... You see, I don't remember." He stopped again and looked at the door and back at Ginger. Then after another moment he said, "I don't remember how I came here. I... in fact I don't remember much from the last few days... or maybe it's been longer."

He stared at Ginger with a look of apprehension. "Please tell me the date."

"It's the twenty-fifth of April," Ginger said.

The man stared at the floor and ran both hands through his hair. "Bloody hell. It's happened again."

GINGER HAD HEARD of people having short-term loss of memory, mostly after being on a drinking binge or something similar. She wondered if this man had spent the last few days passed out from an overindulgence in alcohol or drugs.

Felicia's desk sat perpendicular to Ginger's, where she could observe without being watched. When the investigative work was slow, she spent her time writing mystery novels with the black high-backed typewriter that sat prominently on her desk. But whatever she had been working on before the handsome stranger had stepped in was temporarily forgotten. Felicia, wearing a floral-patterned rayon frock with a modern hemline that ended daringly at the knees, circled around to get a closer look at the man. There was a puzzled look on her face as if she too had seen him before but couldn't quite place him.

"Simpson... yes, it's Simpson," the man said, sitting up straight as a recollection hit. "Mr. Alex Simpson."

Felicia drew in a sharp breath. "You mean the film actor?"

"I—I don't know," the man said. "Perhaps."

Ginger slapped her knee. "I knew I'd seen you somewhere before! My husband and I saw your latest film, *The Pirates of the Aegean Sea*, at the Cameo Theatre last month. It was wonderful!" She looked up at Felicia and then back at the actor. "You look a little less... like a buccaneer at the moment." More like a puppy caught out in a storm, she thought to herself.

"I saw you in *The Brothers Jones* last year," Felicia said. "I thought you did a masterful job of it. By Jove, we have a real celebrity here!"

Felicia flashed a seductive smile and Ginger noted the added sway of her hips as she returned to her desk. Perhaps Felicia's grandmother, the Dowager Lady Gold, was right in insisting that the time had come to find a suitable husband for Felicia. Alas, thanks to the Great War and the way it had culled many young British soldiers, finding eligible men Ambrosia would approve of had been made rather difficult.

Ginger brought her attention back to the baffling case before her.

"Do you remember your work in films?" she asked. Mr. Simpson, according to a movie magazine she'd recently perused, had a reputation for being a real man about town, debonair and polished. Popular with the ladies, he was often cast in leading roles as a dashing figure. It was hard to reconcile that reputation with the unshaven, soggy, and dishevelled man who was slumped in Ginger's chair.

The actor nodded, "Yes."

How odd, Ginger thought. Did the gentleman suffer from selective amnesia?

"Has this happened before?" she asked.

Mr. Simpson slowly ducked his chin. "I'm afraid so. Twice actually. The first one was right after the war when I returned home. Our last offensive was at Cambrai. I was bloody lucky to get out alive. At any rate, six months after my return to London I suddenly found myself in a pub in Croydon with no memory of how I'd got there or what I was doing. I had somehow lost two days. It was terrifying."

Ginger inclined her head. "Are you much of a drinker, Mr. Simpson?" she asked gently.

Their guest shook his head. "Despite what the rags would have you believe, no. I can assure you this event isn't the result of a common drunken stupor."

"Did you consult a doctor the last time?" Felicia asked.

"Yes, Miss Gold, I did. He called it short-term amnesia and referred me to a psychiatrist who, in turn, referred me to a hypnotist." He added bitterly, "Neither was of any help at all."

"I see," Ginger said. To Felicia she added, "I think we could all use a cup of tea."

Felicia departed somewhat reluctantly, but Ginger thought that with the starry-eyed way Felicia was staring, her gaze might just cut the back of their new client's head.

Boss whined, reminding her of his presence.

"Oh, Bossy. Do come and meet our guest." Ginger scooped her pet into her arms and walked around the desk.

"Do you like dogs, Mr. Simpson?"

"Quite."

"This is Boss. He's incredibly friendly. Would you like to pat him?"

Alex Simpson instantly relaxed as he gave Boss much-appreciated affection. A hint of a smile tugged at the corners of his mouth, and in that moment Ginger glimpsed the film star.

Felicia returned with the tea tray and Ginger placed Boss on the woollen rug in his wicker basket.

"Milk and sugar, Mr. Simpson?" Felicia asked.

"Please," the man responded, and received the offered teacup and saucer gratefully.

Once everyone was settled, Mr. Simpson continued, "It seems that short-term amnesia is a mystery to much of the medical community, at least it was almost ten years ago when I first experienced this. The second episode occurred three years ago—I witnessed a bad motorcar crash—with similar results—two calendar days gone and me sitting on a park bench in Piccadilly. I was unhurt, but thoroughly rattled. It appeared that I hadn't slept or eaten during that whole time. At least this time I'm not famished, so I must have eaten something."

Ginger pushed out her lush, painted lips in a pout. "It must be awful to live with the fear that an amnesic episode could happen again at any time."

Mr. Simpson stared at both of them and then down at his right foot. He raised the cuff of his trouser leg, rolled down his argyle sock, and revealed a swollen and discoloured ankle. "I've twisted it somehow, and in addition, I seem to have lost almost two and a half days."

"Felicia?" Ginger started. "Can you please fetch a towel and wet it with cold water." While Felicia disappeared, Ginger retrieved a footstool she had under her desk and placed it in front of Mr. Simpson. He removed his shoe and sock and Ginger noted that the swelling was not severe, but still enough to cause a good amount of pain. Felicia returned with the wet towel and handed it to Mr. Simpson who placed it on his foot.

He leaned back in his chair. "Most kind of you."

"Please tell me everything you do remember," Ginger said.

"I was at *Clapham Studios* finishing a long day of shooting for the forthcoming production of *The Untold War,* a film based on the stories of the unsung heroes of the war. I was looking forward to a much-needed break and planned to drive to the sea for a few days.

"Anyway, I was in my dressing room gathering my things. . . And the next thing I remember I was hobbling down your street in the rain with this sprained ankle, feeling lost and confused. It takes a few minutes for my memory to come back again, and at first I can't even remember my name until I concentrate. After a while, my long-term memory returns. Then, as I said, I read your sign on the door and, well, I guess at this point I am grasping at straws." Mr. Simpson sighed and closed his eyes.

"This is most unusual," Ginger said, sharing a look with Felicia.

Mr. Simpson's eyes snapped open. "Do you think you can help me?" Locking his gaze on Ginger, he added, "You're an investigator, aren't you? And I need someone to help me find out what I've been doing over the last two days. I know it's a desperate thing to do, but perhaps if someone could help me fill in the blanks, my mind would snap out of it and perhaps these... incidents would stop." He looked at her imploringly. "Please, will you help?"

2

_____

$\mathcal{T}$he rain from the day before had abated and the sun's rays shone through the large French doors of the morning room that opened up onto the patio overlooking the back garden at Hartigan House.

Ginger shared a breakfast of eggs, toast, and porridge with her husband, Chief Inspector Basil Reed. His work for the CID kept him busy with murders and dangerous crimes, while Ginger's investigative work tended to be less serious; however, their paths had crossed on more than one occasion and they often had the opportunity to work together. Ginger relayed the account of her new client's unusual mystery, in hopes that her husband might be able to shed a bit of light on it. "Darling, have you ever heard of such a thing?"

"Believe it or not, I have," Basil said as he took a sip of coffee. "I'm familiar with a similar case involving a Boer War soldier. Apparently, it's rather rare. Some medical doctors have used the term '_Fugue State_' to describe it."

"'_Faire une fugue_' is French for 'running away'," Ginger said. She was rather good with languages, a skill that had come in handy while she worked with the British Secret Service in France.

Basil continued, "Some subjects who are in this so-called Fugue State are fully conscious and yet may have no idea who they are. They are confused and highly susceptible to wandering off somewhere randomly or may even try doing things they don't normally do. Others walk around like they are sleepwalking, which is rather dangerous, especially if they decide to drive a motorcar. At the same time, they are able to navigate using buses or the underground. Very odd."

"But you have never come across a case like this personally, I gather," Ginger said.

"No, that would be quite a coincidence if I had, given how rare this is, but as I mentioned, there is one case the police followed of a former soldier from the Boer War, a decorated war hero, actually. He returned from the battlefields in Africa and a few months later stumbled into a police station unshaven, his clothes in tatters, bruises on his face and arms. He claimed he had lost his recent memory. Upon investigation, the police found that he had indeed disappeared from his workplace, and hadn't gone home to his wife and family for three days. The police were baffled and never discovered anything about his whereabouts or his activities during the time of his memory loss."

"Oh mercy," Ginger said. The similarities between the two cases were striking. "Did the incident repeat itself?"

"Yes. Fortunately, the man kept coming back to the police and they were able to safely return him home."

"Do the doctors have any clues as to what causes this bizarre malady?"

Basil stabbed a piece of bacon with his fork. "I don't think so, love, at least nothing conclusive. There's a theory that it could be caused by severe emotional or mental trauma that leaves a mark on the brain somehow. Perhaps a subconscious need to escape, for example. Then, as time goes on, the subject is prone to similar 'fugues' when faced with an event of a very disturbing nature, especially if it resembles the original event in any way."

Ginger's heart went out to Alex Simpson. How awful to have snippets of your life stolen from you. This case would no doubt be one of the most unorthodox investigations she had ever taken on.

CLAPHAM FILM STUDIOS was located on Cranmer Court in

Clapham. Ginger parked her 1924 Crossley in the motorcar park that was filled with older models from the turn of the century, various types of lorries, and even some unattached horse carriages, then opened the back door to let Boss jump out.

Felicia joined them and mused, "I wonder if these vehicles are being used in Mr. Simpson's new film?"

"Quite possibly."

The expansive studios were built underneath six large red-brick railway arches belonging to a discontinued railway line. Each archway was either used as a large doorway or entry for lorries, or was boarded over with painted brick, and on of these the words "Clapham Studios" had been painted.

Inside, Felicia and Ginger, with Boss tucked under her arm, approached the doorman. "Mr. Simpson has given us permission to visit his dressing room." Ginger handed the man her satiny, white business card that had "Lady Gold Investigations" embossed on it in gold lettering.

The doorman raised a questioning brow and stared at the card disapprovingly. "Mr. Simpson telephoned. It's highly unorthodox, but in this case, I'll allow it." He nodded to the receptionist who watched from his position behind the desk.

They were escorted through a makeshift corridor. It opened onto a film set built to mimic the interior of a French house that had been partially destroyed by German heavy artillery. The furniture in the sitting room was broken, shattered china lay on the floor, and the holes in the wall had realistic-looking blast marks.

Ginger was astounded at the realism. Except for the cameras that were set up along the walls, the room looked entirely authentic. She had more than enough pictures to draw the comparison from—she'd been too many ruined houses in Beau-vais as her alias, Antoinette LaFleur, in search, at times, for bodies, and always for secrets.

All that was missing was the terrible, putrid smell of gunpowder and rotting flesh.

Memories and emotions flooded back for Ginger in a surprising manner. Her first husband, Daniel, had died in France, and it was his face that flashed before her mind's eye.

Boss seemed to sense her melancholy and pressed his damp nose into her neck. Ginger patted his head and whispered, "Thank you, Bossy."

"Oh my, isn't this exciting?" Felicia remarked, completely unaware of the scene's emotional impact on Ginger. "Is it very realistic looking?"

"Indeed," Ginger said solemnly. "It is." Though she appreciated the attention to detail and artistry that the set designers had incorporated, she was eager to leave the place. The war seemed to always follow her, even almost a decade later.

The receptionist led them down another short corridor to where the dressing rooms were located, and pointed to a door.

"This is Mr. Simpson's room."

"Thank you," Ginger said. She wasn't sure if tipping was appreciated, but thought it better to offend by offering than to offend by not doing so. One never knew when one might need the goodwill of a receptionist. She slipped the man a shilling, and he closed his fist and grinned.

Ginger knocked, and on hearing the invitation to enter, pressed on the handle, opening the door.

Felicia's hand flew to her mouth while Ginger let out a small gasp. Alex Simpson was dressed in the full khaki, woollen uniform of a British Army officer circa 1915, complete with brass buttons, forage cap, puttee leggings, sidearm revolver, and ammunition boots. Never had Ginger guessed that she would one day once again be standing in front of a soldier from the Great War. Her mouth went dry and her knees turned to liquid. It was like she had entered H.G. Wells' Time Machine and gone back a decade without any warning. Mr. Simpson's facial resemblance to Daniel's was minimal, but nonetheless Ginger knew that Felicia was also wrestling with the emotion of being faced with the striking memory of her brother, Ginger's lost husband, Daniel Gold. For a few moments, the two ladies were speechless.

"You look like you've both seen a ghost." The actor's roguish smile faded. "Erm…Please come in."

3

*G*inger and Felicia stared at Alex Simpson for a moment, until finally Boss wiggled out of Ginger's arms, breaking the spell. They claimed two chairs while Boss settled himself on the rug. A large mirror trimmed with three lights took up one wall. On the dressing table were brushes for applying make up, and several dishes filled with coloured greasepaints. Along with a leather sofa, the room contained a small sink and a large wardrobe with one door ajar revealing various costumes and footwear.

Alex Simpson limped over to the wicker chair and lowered himself into it. Now that the initial shock of seeing a man in a soldier's uniform had worn off, Ginger noticed Mr. Simpson's face was made up with greasepaint, eyeliner, and thickly painted eyebrows.

"Isn't it unusual to be making a film about the war?" Felicia asked tentatively as she looked around the room.

"Well, it has been eight years," said Alex Simpson. "And it's bound to happen sometime. It'll be interesting to see how this film does with the public. Are they ready to relive the war? The directors and producers certainly hope so. Although," he added after a pause, "the writers were compelled to change the names of real soldiers and spies in order to comply with regulations to do with national security. British spies that survived the war are

not allowed to reveal anything about their involvement behind
enemy lines. The Official Secrets Act makes talking about one's
experiences a punishable offence."

Ginger kept her expression blank. She was well acquainted
with the nuances of the Official Secrets Act.

"There are things I'm only learning about now, of course. The
average *Tommy boy* like me knew nothing of things like espionage
and other such secrets."

Ginger was eager to change the subject. "If you don't mind,
before we can really go any further with your case, we need to
ask you a few questions to give us some sort of starting point."

"Of course. I have just now finished filming my bits for the
day, so I have time."

Boss roused himself, padded over to Ginger and jumped onto
her lap.

"I think it might be prudent to check with some of your
friends," Ginger said, patting Boss as he settled into a ball. "And
those in your social circle."

"I've already done that. In fact, I spent the whole evening last
night speaking on the telephone. No one here at the studio, nor
anyone else that I could think of to ring, has seen me since I was
here in my dressing room, almost five days ago now. Of course
they were all a little bewildered at the line of questioning. It's an
embarrassing thing to ask a friend if he has seen one lately. I also
have to be careful because I don't want this in the press." He
reached over to the counter and picked up a towel. "Do you
mind? This stuff can start getting uncomfortable."

"Not at all."

Turning to the mirror, he started spreading cold cream on his
face "Please, continue…"

"Do you have family, Mr. Simpson?" Ginger asked.

"My mother and younger sister both live in Newcastle. My
father was a land speculator and did quite well until he died of a
heart attack while I was serving in France. I rang them last night.
They don't know that I've had these incidents in the past so I had
to be a bit cagey with them. However, my sister answered the
phone with, 'What a surprise! Haven't seen you in months!' so I

knew straightaway I hadn't somehow travelled there during my lapse."

Mr. Simpson cleaned his face as he continued, "It would have been very difficult to get to Newcastle and back anyway during that missing time period."

"I assume you own a motorcar?"

"Yes, I have a Bentley. I found it here parked at the studio this morning. Wherever I went in the last few days, it was via public transport."

"What about places that you frequent?" Felicia asked. "Is there a restaurant, pub, or social club that you like to go to?"

"I'm rather fond of an Italian restaurant in Soho called *Bello Italiano.*"

Felicia, who'd been taking notes, jotted down the name.

"There is also the *South London Golf Club*. I play golf there about once a month or whenever I can find the time to drive there. The club manager knows me well. That's about all I can think of. I know my reputation is a little more... extensive than that, but in fact, I am a bit of a homebody. It's a wonder I've never been married." He winked at Felicia's reflection as he said this, which produced one of Felicia's trademark brilliant smiles in return.

Ginger felt a mild sense of alarm. Mr. Alex Simpson had most definitely come out of his Fugue State! She'd have to have a word with Felicia once they were back at the office. Not only was it bad form to flirt with a client, one had to be extra careful regarding men who had a reputation as charmers.

"What about the place where you live?" Ginger asked, attempting to keep the interview professional. "Is there a care-taker or someone who might have seen you?"

Alex Simpson shook his head. "I've already spoken to the caretaker. Apparently he hasn't seen me in over a week."

"Is there anything else you can think of?" Ginger added. "I don't mean to pry, but if you want us to help you with this we do need to know a few things that are a bit personal."

"Not at all...not at all." Mr. Simpson turned his chair around, his face pink from scrubbing off the greasepaint. "I trust you ladies will be discreet. I'm sure you have to be in your line of work."

"You can rest assured anything you tell us, or any personal elements of this investigation, will not be shared with anyone," Ginger said, "unless it breaks the law. In which case, we are compelled to go to the police."

Alex Simpson reached over and rubbed Boss' head. "What about you, me old mucker?" he said in a mock cockney accent. "I'll bet an 'andsome boyo like you can keep it under your 'at?"

Boss' stump wagged furiously. Mr. Simpson leaned back in his chair and let out a long breath.

"There's a burlesque club in Soho. Once or twice a month I like to go there…that's not a secret. I think it has even been mentioned in the press a few times." He looked at them both as if expecting some kind of reaction, and seemed surprised when it wasn't forthcoming. Ginger and Felicia weren't strangers to the world of the burlesque. In fact, Ginger had once posed as a burlesque dancer as part of a murder investigation.

"It's called *The Goodfellow's Cabaret* on Dean Street," Alex Simpson offered.

A bit of an ironic name, thought Ginger. That was where they would start.

4

_____

$\mathcal{L}$ater that night, Ginger and Felicia entered the front entrance of *The Goodfellow's Cabaret*, looking for a sign of Alex Simpson. The room had dim, red-tinted lighting, plush carpeting, and a noisy ambience, and it was filled with people dressed in the latest fashion. Ginger wore a cheeky pale-yellow low-back gown, which was covered in sequins that sparkled in the candlelight. She had matched it with long white gloves and a rhinestone-studded hair piece that kept her red locks off a carefully painted face. Felicia looked stunning in a sea-green and blue satin affair which she highlighted with a feathery white boa. The ratio of men to women was almost equal, which was not too surprising as most clubs did have a reputation for attracting both sexes.

On the far right was a bar where a large middle-aged, dark-skinned man dispensed drinks. A red-curtained wooden stage with *"The Lucky Lingerie Review"* painted in large letters above it took the back wall. On stage right was a musicians' pit with drums and piano, and a tuba which was leaning against a chair. Young women dressed in skimpy outfits were taking orders at the tables and carrying trays of drinks.

Alex Simpson waved from a corner table, and Ginger and Felicia joined him. After they had ordered drinks he said, "The owner of the place knows me, and several of the girls do as well.

17

I haven't had a chance to talk to any of them yet. You know, I could have just come here by myself and got the information." He smiled crookedly at Felicia. "Or are you amenable to these kinds of places yourself sometimes?"

Felicia smiled back flirtatiously. "No, not usually, but my sister-in-law and I have had occasion to visit a similar club in the course of our investigations."

"Oh?" He raised one eyebrow and leaned forward a bit towards Felicia. "Do tell me."

"At any rate," Ginger cut in. She didn't want this conversation to get sidetracked, and she had absolutely no desire to discuss her own talent as a burlesque performer, or to watch Felicia fall under this charismatic man's spell. Ginger continued on, "It helps to have an objective party ask the questions and observe the subject as he or she answers." During the war, Ginger had undertaken training in how to read things like facial expressions and bodily movements. These skills had saved her life on more than one occasion and been very helpful in past investigations. In the case of Mr. Simpson's missing memory, she didn't know yet if any crime had been committed, but if there had, someone along the way was likely to try to lie about it.

Mr. Simpson opened his mouth to comment on that but just then the piano player struck up a rousing tune and the curtain opened to reveal a thin man in a suit and top hat. He walked quickly and jauntily to the front of the stage, swinging his arms in an exaggerated fashion, and then faced the audience. The piano stopped playing and the man cleared his throat.

"This is usually the warm-up act before the dancers take the stage," Alex Simpson explained unnecessarily.

The man on the stage took off his hat and said, "Hello. Oh no, ladies, I'm not Buster Keaton!" He had an American accent and spoke in a nasal voice. "Dear old Buster hasn't got nearly the good looks that I have." The crowd hooted in laughter. "It's funny though, for a man as handsome as me, I usually get the homeliest girls. Plain, but nice, mind you. I just quit my last girl... family had a lot of troubles. Her poor father died of a throat malady." He paused for effect. "They hanged him."

At this, the crowd roared again. This went on for about five minutes and the performer ended in a silly song about a seasick seagull named Winthrop. Felicia and Mr. Simpson both found the act funny and laughed heartily at every quip. Ginger managed to smile at some of them, but was glad when the curtain closed and the man disappeared.

Ginger noticed one of the serving girls staring at Mr. Simpson as she went about her duties. This in itself was not so unusual, given his celebrity status, but the girl wore a perplexed expression on her pretty face, as if she were puzzled that Mr. Simpson was there sitting at a table in the club. Finally she came over, shot Ginger and Felicia a suspicious glance, then put her serving tray on the table and slid in next to Mr. Simpson. She wore heavy makeup, strong, cheap perfume, and a headband with a wilting black plume.

"Alex, I'm so surprised to see you 'ere so soon."

"Oh, hello... uh, Julia, is it? No." He chuckled. "It's June. How are you, June? How's the new job coming along here?"

"Well, it's goin' as well as a girl can expect. Some of the men can be a bother, but I manage all right, I reckon. 'Oo are your friends then?" She smiled at Ginger and Felicia but it carried no warmth.

"This is Mrs. Reed and her sister Miss Gold. They are, erm... helping me with a certain..."

"So pleased to meet you, Miss June," Ginger interrupted. "My sister and I are old friends of the Simpson family. Why, I knew Alex when he was just a young lad back on Tyneside. Back then his Geordie accent was much more noticeable, of course."

"Oooee," the young woman squealed. "Blimey, how adorable! Can I hear some o' that?"

"Eeeh, lass, ahm gannin doon the boozer. Yer knaa what ah mean, leik?" he said out of the corner of his mouth like an old sailor.

The young lady laughed out loud, then put her arm under his while sidling closer to him.

"Why are you surprised to see him here?" Ginger asked.

June's face was suddenly serious and she looked first at Ginger and then at Mr. Simpson. "Well, I don't know if I should..."

"No worries, my dear, you can say anything to these two," Mr. Simpson said. "No secrets here."

"Well, it's just—" June's eyes betrayed her inner deliberation.

"Go on," Alex Simpson encouraged her.

"All right," June said. "Your aunt, Mrs Woodbury, told me that it usually takes at least three days to recover from one of your drinking binges, and that you would stay at The Dunsbury Manor for the remainder of the week."

Mr. Simpson stared at the serving girl, then shrugged in Ginger's direction. He mouthed, "I don't know her."

Back to the girl he said, "June, be a dear and excuse us for a moment, will you?" When he saw the look of alarm on her face he added, "Don't worry, you've done nothing wrong. Please come back with another round of drinks."

June shrugged and left with her serving tray.

"It seems our case might be solved," Ginger said with a pointed look at her client.

"Not quite yet," he returned. Leaning forward, he looked at them both. "I don't have any aunts at all, much less one by the name of Woodbury, and as far as my admittedly leaky memory serves me, I am actually not a heavy drinker and furthermore I have never smoked, swallowed, or otherwise ingested any illicit drugs in my entire life."

He swallowed as his eyes darted to their waitress. "I don't know why she would, but our girl June is lying."

5

-----

*W*hen June returned with a second round of drinks, Mr. Simpson asked her to sit down again. She shot a questioning glance at Felicia and Ginger before complying.

"If you don't mind," Ginger said, "we need to ask you a question or two that might seem strange."

June nodded, looking a bit uncertain. "Erm…all right."

"When did you meet Mr. Simpson's aunt?"

"Well, a few days ago, wasn't it?" She looked at Mr. Simpson. "It was when you came in 'ere all cocked up on whisky. You could barely put two words together, luv. Don't you remember?"

He stared back sheepishly. "I'm afraid not, my dear."

"Oh, then that explains a thing or two, don't it?" June shook her head at Ginger while rolling eyes under their heavily painted lashes. "You come in 'ere and sat down all by yourself at that table over there." The waitress pointed to a smaller table in the opposite corner of the room. "You looked lost and lonely, so I come and sat wiv you for a few minutes. You weren't much for talkin' though. When I got up, a lady called me over to 'er table. She was a bit out of place here, mind you. Definitely not our normal customer, at least fifty years old, and not 'xactly a flapper. She tol' me you were 'er nephew and she wanted to make sure you got 'ome safe. But she said you was bein' stubborn and wanted to come 'ere instead."

"Can you describe her?" Ginger asked.

June worked her deep red lips. "I didn't see 'er face that well, to be honest. She 'ad on an 'at with a black veil covering 'alf of 'er face the way some ladies do. But she wore a black dress which looked pretty expensive to me, I'll say. That's about all I can tell ya. It's dark in 'ere as you can see… and a lot of smoke. I couldn't even tell you the colour of 'er 'air under 'er 'at, 'cept it wasn't blonde."

"What else did she tell you?" Felicia asked.

June looked at Mr. Simpson. "She wanted me to take you to your place at The Dunsbury Manor. She said it was the room you 'ad there permanent so you could go an' clear your 'ead when you needed to be anonymous, like."

Mr. Simpson looked at Ginger with wide eyes. He shook his head from side to side slowly.

"Didn't you think that was a bit odd?" Felicia asked.

"*Very* odd!" June agreed. "Blimey, I thought the ol' lady was off her bean. But then she said she'd give me twenty quid, *twenty quid!* That's rich, innit?" She shook her head again. "Ol' aunty told me that 'e wouldn't follow '*er* to the 'otel but that 'e would go with a pretty girl like me, especially since we were friends already."

"June?" Ginger started, making sure to have the girl's full attention. "Did you take Mr. Simpson to The Dunsbury Manor?"

"Of course I did. I just sat down beside 'im an' after a bit I asked if he wanted to go 'ome wiv me. He just looked at me and nodded 'is head real slow-like. Poor dearie. Now I'm no trollop, am I? I didn't try nuffin' with you, luv." She took Mr. Simpson's hand and kissed him on the cheek. "Not that I would be opposed to somefin', but not when you're barely breathin'. You didn't say a word the 'ole way there. You must 'ave taken more than your share of the ol' *Dover's powder* that night. Anyway, she gave me a key to your room. We took a taxi there, it's not far."

"What happened then?" Ginger asked.

"As I said, nuffin' much. In fact, Mrs. Woodbury gave me strict instructions *not* to stay in the room. I just opened the door, we stepped in, and I gave 'im a big kiss and left. From the look on your face, you thought I was goin' ta stay, didn't you, luv?" She gave Mr. Simpson another kiss on the cheek.

"And the key?" Ginger asked.

"Mrs. Woodbury tol' me to lock the door an' leave the key 'angin on the outside so she could check on 'im later, make sure 'e was okay."

"Did you see anyone at the hotel?" Felicia asked. "A night receptionist, perhaps?"

"No one. The 'otel has a separate entrance if you already 'ave your key."

"Do you remember the room number?" Mr. Simpson asked.

"Well, course I do, luv, but don't *you*?" she looked at him strangely. He grinned and winked, but didn't reply.

"What is the number please?" Ginger prodded.

"Well, it's twenty-six, innit?" June said, obviously flabbergasted by the question.

Ginger shifted out of her chair. "We must go there immediately."

IT WAS NEARING ten o'clock by the time they reached The Dunsbury Manor on Dunsbury Street. The elegant hotel was painted white with gold trim on the window and door frames, and stood five storeys high. The first floor had one continuous balcony that extended along the front while the upper floor windows each had their own small balcony, wrapped in black wrought iron railings which held beautiful pots with exotic-looking flowers. Ginger had driven past the distinctive-looking hotel many times, but had never been inside. She, Felicia, and Mr. Simpson, still limping and now using a cane, crossed the expansive, marble floor of the reception room and approached the receptionist's desk.

"Hello, my good fellow," Mr. Simpson said to the kindly looking middle-aged man wearing a receptionist's black and red uniform.

The man smiled back. "My name is Willoughby. Do you have a reservation?"

Mr. Simpson leaned on the counter. "You mean to say you

don't know me? I have a room here booked already, and have had for quite some time. I'm afraid I've lost my key though. Can you be a good chap and give me a second one?"

"Of course, sir, I do recognise you, Mr. Simpson," the man said apologetically. "In fact my wife and I are avid filmgoers. We have seen your last two pictures. I didn't realise you had a room at our hotel. What an honour to have you here. I'm not here every day so I must have missed your name on the ledger."

As the receptionist searched the ledger, his face registered confusion. "I don't see your name listed, Mr. Simpson. Can I please have your room number?"

With a glance at Ginger, Alex Simpson answered, "Twenty-six."

Mr. Willoughby stared back with a startled expression. "Room twenty-six is not in use, sir. That section of the hotel has been closed for nearly a year now due to smoke damage from an old fire, still dirty and smelly. There must be a mistake. Erm… just let me search for your name again." He turned a few pages and ran his finger down a list of names. He then turned one more page and checked it as well. Finally he looked up and smiled apologetically, "I am sorry but I don't see your name registered. You say you've had the room for a while? When did you first check in, sir?"

Ginger stepped up to the counter. "I am sorry sir, we didn't want to mislead you but we thought it might be necessary to gain certain information. I am Lady Gold from Lady Gold Investigations. My husband is Chief Inspector Basil Reed at Scotland Yard. This is my assistant, Miss Gold."

She handed her business card to the receptionist and his eyes widened in surprise.

"We are here on a rather urgent matter to do with Mr. Simpson and a possible criminal case."

"Oh dear me," the man returned. His rotund cheeks bloomed red. "Nothing serious, I hope." His small eyes darted about the lobby as he lowered his voice. "Bad press is bad for business."

Ginger gave the man a kind but pointed look. "If you wouldn't mind terribly, please show us that room?"

He looked at the card for a long moment and then at the three of them. "Yes, all right, then. But I can assure you, no one has been in there for several months. Let me just get the key and I can show you the entrance door." He returned in less than a minute and led them outside. "The access to that part of the building is by a separate door at the back," he said. "The usual entrance through the hotel is closed off."

"May I ask who owns the hotel?" Felicia said.

"It is owned by the Williams brothers of Liverpool, along with six other fine hotels in London and Manchester. None of the brothers has been here in person since the fire." Mr. Willoughby led them around the building to a dimly lit area facing a back alley.

Noticing Alex Simpson's limp, the receptionist enquired, "Is your leg all right, sir? It's not far."

"I'll be fine," Mr. Simpson answered. "Lead on."

Mr. Willoughby unlocked a door that opened to a staircase. He felt for a light switch and the stairs lit up. "Sorry, there is no lift operating here right now; can you manage, Mr. Simpson?"

"I'll manage fine, thank you."

"Here's the key to the room." He handed it to Ginger. "I'll leave you here since I have to go back to reception. The man who is normally on duty tonight is ill. We have a guest here, a Mrs. Farnhurst, who always comes to pick up her post from the front desk at precisely fifteen minutes past ten." He looked at his watch, "She tends to get cross if her post hasn't already been sorted. Please lock up when you've finished. The room you're looking for will be facing the back of the building on the second floor. I doubt if you will find anything. That room should be completely empty." He turned and hurried away.

Alex Simpson struggled with the stairs, gripping the bannister tightly.

"Oh, let me help you," Felicia offered.

A round of giggling ensued and Ginger rolled her eyes. After some effort they made it to the right floor. There was a mild scent of smoke from the carpet, and dust and a few cobwebs gathered in the corners. The trio quickly found the room. Mr. Simpson took a deep breath as Ginger inserted the key into the lock.

"Wait a moment, please," Alex Simpson said. "I've never

knowingly gone back to a place where I spent time during a memory lapse. I must admit my heart is beating like a drum. There's no way of knowing if my memory will come flooding back or not, and..." The colour had drained from his face.

"You'll be fine," Felicia said with a smile. She clasped his hand and continued encouragingly. "We can't very well turn back now, can we?"

"No, I suppose not."

Ginger opened the door.

6

The room was sparsely furnished and the air contained a curious aromatic mixture of smoke and basil, as if someone had made an effort to cover the smell of smoke with herbs. Darkened paint smudges rimmed the top of the wallpapered walls and parts of the ceiling.

It appeared as if someone had dusted and cleaned the room recently, but it wasn't professionally done. There were still cobwebs in some of the ceiling corners and a thin layer of dust could be seen on the small bedside table. The bed had recently been slept in; the covers were still in disarray. A large window faced a dark street. On a small table in the centre of the bedroom sat a large, half-empty bottle of expensive-looking Rémy Martin brandy. Beside it was an empty glass and a handwritten note.

Like a man in a dream, Mr. Simpson limped over to the table. He sat down and slowly looked around the room. "I... remember this."

Ginger picked up the note which was written on plain white paper, obviously in fountain pen. *My dear boy,* it said, *I am terribly sorry for trapping you in here, but everything will be all right. I'll come to visit very soon and explain everything. We'll have wonderful talks which we both shall enjoy greatly, I am sure. You'll be glad for my company. In the meantime, please enjoy this fine brandy.*

The note was unsigned.

Mr. Simpson reached for the glass beside the Rémy Martin bottle. "I need a drink, all right."

"Stop," Ginger said. "I suspect that brandy is drugged."

Mr. Simpson slowly withdrew his hand. "Yes, it must be. I do remember bits and pieces now. I remember waking up here." He got up and sat down on the edge of the bed and lay back. He put both his hands to his temples and then sprung upright. "I woke up very groggy, yes, just as if I were drugged." He looked again at the brandy bottle. "Then I went to the door, but it was locked from the outside." Pointing vaguely, he continued, "I pounded and yelled, but no one came. There's a gap in my memory then… I don't know what happened next. Oh wait, I think I eventually went to the window. It was raining."

Alex Simpson moved from the bed to the window and fussed with the handle. The window swung open. Ginger and Felicia joined him, one on either side, and stared out over the two floors down to the street below.

To escape through the window, one would have to climb out onto a small ledge, then, using the steel brackets that attached the large drainpipe to the building, climb down to the flat roof of the adjacent building. Then, one would have to swing down to one of the window ledges and jump the final distance to the cobblestones below. It would be possible to negotiate the entire journey from the window to the ground if one were fit, but it would be complicated, especially if one's mind wasn't clear.

"I think that explains your injury," Ginger said, nodding towards Alex Simpson's injured leg. "You must have stumbled your way somehow to our office from here."

"Though the studio doesn't like it, I insist on doing my own stunts," Mr. Simpson said. "Funny thing though, I have no memory of this, nor of walking to your office. My next memory is standing in front of your door in the rain."

Ginger tested the handle of a door that opened easily to an adjoining room. It was half the size of the bedroom with a fireplace and a much smaller window.

"This might've been used as a sitting room," Ginger said. "Hang on, what's this?" Over the fireplace and down each side, there were dozens of photographs and cut-out pages from magazines pinned to the wall. There were two small tables with large candles underneath the photos. It looked like a shrine.

The pictures were all of Alex Simpson. There were publicity photos, shots from film magazines with editorial writings about him, and a few other photos of varying quality clearly taken from a distance.

Felicia gasped.

Mr. Simpson whispered, "What in heaven's name?"

GINGER STEPPED CLOSER to the photo-covered wall and picked up a small photograph. It was the only one that did not seem to be of Alex Simpson, but rather someone who looked very similar—a younger, stouter version of Alex Simpson. The hair appeared to be the same shade, but the eyes were set wider apart and were framed by wire spectacles.

The portrait photograph must have been taken during the period of the Great War by a professional photographer. Taken from the waist up, the subject was dressed in a soldier's uniform and wore a field cap. Ginger turned the photo over. In blue ink was written on the back *'We will see each other again someday. Rest in Peace-1918'*. Ginger put the photograph into her handbag.

"This is now definitely a criminal case, Mr. Simpson," Ginger said. "You are a victim of kidnapping. I suggest that you inform the police."

"I would rather keep this a private matter, Mrs. Reed. If the press were to learn that I was having memory lapses it would be terrible publicity for both myself and the film studios. I am confident in your abilities as an investigator."

"In that case," Ginger said as if she had already anticipated Mr. Simpson's response, "I would still like to inform my husband at Scotland Yard. Eventually, when we do get to the bottom of this, we may need his help in apprehending the suspect and to make the arrest. I can assure you he will be discreet."

"Very well," Mr. Simpson said.

Felicia pivoted on her T-strap shoe. "What do we do next?"

"Fortunately, we now have some clues to go on," Ginger replied. "We have a description of a lady in her fifties who is obviously obsessed with Mr. Simpson. She may be well-to-do or at least well enough to wear a fashionable dress and buy expensive brandy. We have a photograph taken during the war of someone who looks a lot like Mr. Simpson. Last but not least," Ginger tapped on her handbag, "we have a handwritten note and the handwriting on the back of this photograph."

"What good will that do?" Mr. Simpson asked.

"I happen to have some knowledge of graphology," Ginger said. The study of handwriting analysis had been included in the training she received as a spy during the war. "We can analyse the handwriting and compare it with other examples to determine a match."

"Yes, like fingerprints," Mr. Simpson said.

"It is not always as accurate as that, I'm afraid," Ginger answered. "However, it does work a lot of the time. It is extremely rare for two people to have exactly the same handwriting patterns. If you know where to look, you can very often match handwriting samples on two documents that were written by the same person."

"How fascinating," Felicia said with wide-eyed interest.

"Now then," Ginger said with a clap of her hands. "We'll also need to find out how the suspect gained access to this room. But first things first."

Ginger felt invigorated. Until now, this case had yielded very few clues and her initial fears of taking it on had seemed to be well founded. But now she was quickly gaining confidence that the case could very well be solved.

"Mr. Simpson, can you think of anyone who would fit the description of the lady that June described? Someone who is on the periphery of your circle of friends perhaps?"

He thought for a moment. "There is a lady who, together with her husband, owns a catering company called *Food Corps*. That company serves Clapham Studios during filming projects. She is about that age, I think. Her name is Mrs. Westcott. She is always very friendly to me when she comes to check on her workers and has told me that she reads every newspaper article written about me." He snapped his fingers, his expression lightening as if he had suddenly remembered something. "By Jove, she once told me that I remind her of her son who died in the war…"

"That's something," Ginger said. "Anyone else?"

"Yes, there is a photographer for *The Film Gazette.*"

This was of interest to Ginger as several of the photos on the wall of the small hotel sitting room were pages torn from a popular film enthusiasts' magazine.

"Her name is Miss Findlay," Mr. Simpson continued. "Even though she is formally retired from photography she keeps showing up at almost every party and every film promotional gala, snapping pictures of me. Quite honestly, she's annoying. Once I caught her taking pictures while I was having dinner at The Barclay *on the Strand* with a lady friend. Appalling behaviour, even for a magazine photographer."

"That may also be useful," Ginger agreed. "I believe we have a way forward now, but we must move quickly. Whoever tried to keep you in this room has undoubtedly by now discovered that you have escaped, so we must act before the birds can eat the breadcrumbs off the trail, so to speak."

She paced a small circle. "Mr. Simpson, I'll telephone you if and when we need to talk further, but for now you can rest assured your case is in good hands. Felicia and I will continue with the investigation." Holding the brass key in the air, she added, "I'll drop this back at the receptionist's desk. He'll be surprised to know that not only has this room been occupied, but it was used for a kidnapping. He must keep this room guarded and untouched until the police investigate."

"I say," said Mr. Simpson. "Going back to work on the film will seem frightfully boring after sleuthing with you lot."

7

———

$\mathcal{M}$r. and Mrs. Westcott lived in a renovated three-storey detached Victorian house in south-east London. The bottom two floors had broad, freshly painted wooden frames around large bay windows and the front door. The top floor had two smaller windows under the double gables with colourful potted plants attached to the small iron railings that hung beneath. As Ginger parked her motorcar and crossed the street, she was struck by how cheerful looking the house was; like something out of a children's storybook. Parked on the street near the house was a green food van with *"Food Corps—Proudly Serving the Greater London Area"* painted in gold lettering on the sides.

This morning, Ginger had chosen to wear a business-like pale-grey two-piece suit consisting of a box coat and narrow wrap-around skirt. She wanted to convey the look of a woman who was here as part of her job rather than on a social call. For this reason, she had once again left Boss at home under the care of Scout, her adopted son. Scout and Boss had become fast friends over the last little while and Boss definitely did not seem to mind being left at home at Hartigan House with the lad.

Ginger knocked on the door and was greeted by a middle-aged man dressed very casually in a white cotton shirt and brown woollen trousers held up with black braces. Balding, he

32

had a gruff look about him, although his brown eyes seemed friendly.

"Hello," Ginger said with a slight Irish brogue as she held out her gloved hand. "I'm Miss Flanagan from *The Iron Pages*. You must be Mr. Westcott."

"Yes, hello," the man said as he shook her hand lightly. "Mrs. Westcott told me you would be coming this morning. Please come in."

"Do you run your catering business from your home?" Ginger asked as she took in the small but tastefully decorated entrance hall.

"Mostly," the man said. "We have a large kitchen at the back of the house, and employ cooks to prepare and organise the food. We have drivers who deliver the finished meals to parties, and film and music studios all over London." Mr. Westcott rocked on his toes, his eyes flashing with pride. "My wife and I do all the paperwork and organisation from our office upstairs. We started this business just after the war with just ourselves and one delivery van."

Frightfully impressive, Ginger mused. The Westcotts had done well for themselves without the benefit of a large inheritance, *and* together as a husband and wife team.

Mr. Westcott led her into a cosy sitting room where a plate of biscuits and a tea tray was waiting. A middle-aged lady wearing a simple but stylish cotton dress walked in from a doorway at the other end of the room. She smiled at Ginger and took her gloved hand in both of hers. "Hello there! I'm Mrs. Westcott. You must be the lady who called. You're from that magazine... *The Iron Paper* or something."

"*The Iron Pages,*" Ginger corrected.

"Yes, that's it. Please have a seat." Ginger lowered herself into comfortable leather wingback chair and took out a notebook from her handbag while Mr. and Mrs. Westcott sat on the settee opposite her.

"Well, let's get right to it, shall we?" Ginger continued in a soft brogue, smiling at them. Having lived in both London and Boston for significant portions of her life, Ginger had been exposed to plenty of accents. Boston, in particular, had a large Irish population.

"As I said when I rang you, our magazine is a new enterprise, based in south-east London. We are dedicated to telling the stories of those who hail right here from our district who have lost a daughter or son in the war."

"How wonderful," Mrs. Westcott exclaimed. "I would love to tell you the story of our dear Robert." She looked at her husband who smiled back at her with a hint of sadness.

"I can't promise that we'll print this particular story—we have several pieces in the running—but I'll do my best, and will let you know if we go ahead with it."

A trip to the War Records Department might've got her the information she was looking for, but Ginger had wanted to actually meet the lady. So far however, she did not see any signs of an unbalanced or obsessive personality.

"Our magazine is also following the filming of *The Untold War* which is where I heard about you and your son. I had the privilege of interviewing Mr. Alex Simpson yesterday at Clapham Studios and he told me that you had mentioned a certain resemblance. Do you have a photograph I could see?"

"Of course we do!" Mrs. Westcott moved to a small cabinet where she pulled out a framed portrait picture as well as other smaller images. "I usually have these hanging on the wall, but the maid was cleaning the wallpaper, and I am quite protective of these photographs."

She handed the picture to Ginger who took it carefully. The young man in uniform bore no resemblance whatsoever to Alex Simpson or to the photograph Ginger had taken from the hotel room. The Westcott son was slimmer in build, had a pronounced chin, and light hair. The woman might've been reminded somehow of her deceased son when she saw Alex Simpson in the soldier's costume, just as Ginger and Felicia had been reminded of Daniel. But in both cases, the actual resemblance was weak at best.

"When did he die?" Ginger asked.

Mr. Westcott answered softly. "He was part of the British

Expeditionary Force on the thirteen of September at the first battle at Aisne."

"Nineteen fourteen," Ginger said in a reverent whisper. She placed her hand on the photograph as if to bless the young man in it.

The soldier in the photograph tucked away in Ginger's handbag had died in 1918 according to the writing on its back.

Mrs. Westcott was not the woman in the black veil.

8

———

*G*inger, Felicia, and Alex Simpson sat it the office of Lady Gold Investigations and stared at a small pile of envelopes that the actor had brought with him. Boss was in his usual station in the basket beside the desk, fast asleep. Occasionally he let out a small snoring sound and Ginger would tap him on the head lightly so he would change position. Apparently, spending the morning with Scout had been strenuous for the Boston Terrier.

It was common for film stars to have admirers who wanted to somehow communicate with their favourite celebrity, and this often came in the form of letters and postcards.

"Before we look at these, let's hear from you, Felicia," Ginger said. She'd commissioned Felicia to pose as a student of photography with the School of Photoengraving in Bolt Court, in order to gain a meeting with Miss Findlay, the semi-retired photographer for *The Film Gazette*.

"My heart was beating like a hammer," Felicia started, "but I was easily able to make a quick appointment with her once I told her that I was a long-time admirer of her work. She seemed quite pleased with the idea that she had an admirer. We met for lunch at a small café in Central London and chatted about the latest films, and what her career as a photojournalist has been like." Felicia moved her gaze to Alex Simpson and stared at him from under her eyelashes. "I asked her about you, Mr. Simpson, but she seemed reticent to talk, which surprised me."

Mr. Simpson shifted in his seat. "The last time we spoke it wasn't on pleasant terms."

"Did she mention if she had a son who died in the war?" Ginger asked.

Felicia interrupted. "*Miss* Findlay told me she had never married, so of course there were no children."

"She could be lying about that," Mr. Simpson quickly said. He recrossed his legs. "A woman can easily change her title from Mrs. to Miss to avoid detection, and it's not unheard of for unmarried women to have secret children."

"What name did you use?" Ginger asked. "And perhaps even more importantly, whatever did you wear?"

"I used the name Charlotte Gladwell. Just a name I thought up. Just imagine that!"

Ginger had to smile at Felicia's enthusiasm.

"Oh, you would have loved my outfit! It was a dowdy brown tweed affair together with a boring cloche hat and undecorated pumps."

Ginger nodded with an appraising grin. "Very good!"

"By Jove, you could be an actress," Mr. Simpson added.

At this Felicia turned a bright red, but only for an instant as she coyly replied, "Thank you for the compliment, but I'm afraid the world will have to wait until someone invents a way for me to talk on film before I venture onto the screen. Talking is too important to me."

"Jolly good," he chortled. "Talkies, as the Americans like to call them, are on their way."

As if to punctuate that sentence, Boss let out a big snore. They all looked down at him and chuckled.

Felicia turned to Ginger. "In any case, at the end I asked Miss Findlay to sign my new 'study notebook' that I was going to use for taking notes during lectures at the school. I told her this would inspire me onward to become a true *ace* like her. That's journalism slang that I read about before we had the meeting."

"Were you able to convince her to write down what I told you?"

"Oh yes, yes I was!" Felicia opened her notebook to the first page. "She did find it a bit odd that I wanted her to write these exact words, but in the end she did it."

To Charlotte Gladwell. Very soon you will be leaving the trappings of school and will be joining the ranks of photojournalists. Until then, I hope you have a wonderful time and perhaps we will see each other again. Yours, Esther Findlay.

"I don't understand," Mr. Simpson said. "Why did you want her to write those exact words?"

"Because this small paragraph contains corresponding words we have as samples from the photograph and the handwritten note, in order to compare," Ginger explained. "In this case we have the words *and, very soon, trappings, joining, we will see each other again, until then,* and *wonderful.*"

"Brilliant!" Mr. Simpson stated. "All right then, let's compare."

Ginger studied the notation and shook her head. "No. Look at the way the writer shapes their *e*'s, and the two *p*'s in 'trapping' are joined. These two samples are radically different." Ginger reached out an empty palm. "Now then, let's take a look at your letters, shall we?"

"There were actually quite a few that seemed a bit strange to me," Mr. Simpson said, "but I was able to narrow it down to those that seemed rather pushy and possessive."

Ginger nodded. "Show me the oddest one first please."

"Well, this person wrote two letters." Mr. Simpson handed two envelopes to Ginger who proceeded to open the first one. It didn't have a return address, and the letter itself was written on plain paper.

My dear boy, I was very disappointed to read in the London Times about your recent behaviour. Burlesque? Really, you should be more disciplined and careful with whom you keep company. I have told you before, but you don't seem to listen. You're quite intent on trapping yourself in some sort of bohemian lifestyle and I am terribly afraid you will bring dishonour on yourself.

Just like the note in the hotel, this note was unsigned. Ginger circled the words '*My dear boy, company, you, trapping, terribly,* then opened the second envelope.

My dear boy, I really think you need a good motherly visit soon. I need to explain a few things to you. You continue to do everything in your power to make me sorry to have ever picked up a morning newspaper. Your recent liaison with that American actress is shameful. Expect a visit from me soon.

Ginger and Felicia both looked up at Mr. Simpson.

"She must be referring to Lillian Baxter. She was in London for two days..." He shrugged his shoulders helplessly.

Ginger circled the words, *My dear boy, sorry, explain.*

"Both letters start with the words, *My dear boy,*" Ginger said. "In addition, both letters indicate someone with an obsession. She seems to place herself in the role of a scolding mother."

"I already have one of those," Mr. Simpson said with a grin. "Don't need another."

Ginger took out the photo from the hotel and the note. Even at first glance the writing appeared similar, having the same tight script with its lower loops running into each other. Ginger tapped the corresponding words on each document with her fingernail. They were almost identical. In particular, the *t*'s were all crossed very high on the stems, the *a*'s and *o*'s all had a curious round, rather than oval, shape to them, and the capital *M* in 'My dear boy' was written overly large and with much flourish. The writing was an obvious match.

"No need to go through the other letters," Ginger said. "This is our mystery writer."

Mr. Simpson whistled. "Bloody hell."

"Now if we only had a return address," Ginger said. She picked up both fan letters and idly turned the second one over. "Oh, what's this?" On the back side at the top was a faded letterhead with a stylised eagle's head on the right-hand side. Whoever wrote the letter must have done so in haste without realising that she was writing on the blank side of a sheet of hotel stationery. It said, *"The Woodsbury Hotel, Manchester"*.

"Felicia," Ginger said. "Please ring Scotland Yard."

9
_____

*W*hen Ginger and Basil arrived at Dunsbury Manor later that afternoon, Basil parked the Crossley in front of the building and they both climbed out. Ginger's first telephone call from her office just an hour before had been to *The Woodsbury Hotel* in Manchester. She'd spoken to the manager who had confirmed that the Williams brothers of Liverpool also owned Dunsbury Manor in London.

Basil had rung up the Williams brothers in Liverpool on official police business and was connected to John Williams, the oldest son of the late Henry Williams, a well-known hotelier. He informed Mr. Williams about the kidnapping that had been committed at their London hotel, and that the perpetrator had written a note on the letterhead of The Woodsbury *Hotel* in Manchester. The man was naturally appalled.

The purpose of the call had been to inform the Williams brothers that there was going to be an immediate police search of Dunsbury Manor and that the police would require access to the unused portion of the hotel. Basil also enquired as to who might have a connection to the two hotels, particularly anyone who was a middle-aged woman and a long-term guest.

"We have an aunt from our mother's side," the man reluctantly admitted. The widow, Mrs. Farnhurst, had been living in a large suite on the second floor of Dunsbury Manor for the last fifteen years. "She's a recluse," Mr. Williams had said, "The hotel manager doesn't even know she's related to us in any way."

"The hotel receptionist mentioned her!" Ginger remarked. She remembered how the receptionist had had to hurry back to the reception desk after he had shown them to the hotel room, because the lady grew irritable if her post was not sorted in time. They had missed seeing her in the hotel lobby by only a few minutes!

The night porter that Ginger and Mr. Simpson had met the night before was not there; instead, a younger man with a moustache and spectacles attended the reception desk.

"Good evening," Basil said as he approached. "I'm Chief Inspector Reed from Scotland Yard and this is my consultant, Lady Gold from Lady Gold Investigations. With the Williams brothers' cooperation, we are here on police business and would like to speak to Mrs. Farnhurst. I'm told she lives on the second floor."

"Yes...yes she does." The man stared back with a look of astonishment. "She doesn't go out much, so there's a good chance she is in. Shall I ring her for you?"

"That won't be necessary," Ginger said. "If you can just tell us her room number?"

"Room twenty-eight."

The room bordered the closed-down section of the hotel, not far from where Mr. Simpson had been kept. Ginger, knowing the way, led Basil there. He knocked on the door, but an answer was not immediately forthcoming, so after waiting a few moments, he knocked again and said loudly, "Mrs. Farnhurst? This is Chief Inspector Basil Reed from Scotland Yard. If you are there please open the door."

He was about to knock again when the door suddenly opened. Before them stood a middle-aged lady wearing a simple day frock that hung unfashionably from a generous bosom. She had striking, steel-blue eyes, which stared indignantly at both of them. Her dark hair was streaked with grey and was neatly pinned back in a bun. Her thin, severe-looking mouth was tightened in a defiant scowl, suggesting she already knew why an inspector had suddenly arrived at her door.

Basil removed his hat. "Good evening. Mrs. Farnhurst, I presume?"

"That's right," she answered gruffly.

"As I said, I am Chief Inspector Basil Reed from Scotland Yard and this is my consultant, Lady Gold from Lady Gold Investigations."

Mrs. Farnhurst glanced haughtily at Ginger and then set her gaze back on Basil.

"I'm afraid we have to ask you some questions," Basil replied. "May we come in?"

"Yes, if you must then," Mrs. Farnhurst said with a huff.

The room was similar to 26 but was much more lavishly decorated. Ginger and Basil sat down on two chairs that faced a luxurious brown leather settee which was where Mrs. Farnhurst took a seat.

"You don't mind if I don't offer tea?" she said.

"Not at all," Basil said. He cleared his throat before continuing. "As I understand it, you are an aunt to the Williams brothers, and they have given you this room to live in."

"Yes, their mother was my sister. She was a good woman, married to a good man. It's too bad the brothers have turned out to be such scallywags." She stared ahead with a look of bitterness. "There's no end to their philandering. All three of them act like immature schoolboys. Only one of them, Harold, has found a wife and even he can't seem to keep his thoughts on hearth and home. Thank God that that marriage has not produced children. Appalling behaviour."

Basil and Ginger shared a stunned look.

"But it seems they have been rather generous to you?" Ginger remarked.

"It's the least they could do, I think." The woman raised both eyebrows and shook her head as if Ginger was missing the point.

Basil went straight to it. "Mrs. Farnhurst, why did you go to such elaborate lengths to trick Mr. Simpson into coming to room twenty-six down the corridor and then trap him there? I mean, how did you accomplish it all in the first place?"

Mrs. Farnhurst answered without hesitation. "It's really very simple. I just couldn't bear to see it anymore. That young man has such potential to be an example, with so many eyes upon him. Instead he is wasting his life with sordid affairs. Keeping company with women of ill-repute and men of low moral character. So, I thought it would be splendidly ironic to use that trollop at that disgusting club to lure him here. I simply waited in my car for him outside the film studio. I knew he would go to that awful place. He had obviously already had too much to drink by the way he walked to the taxi." She clicked her tongue. "The drug in the brandy was simply a bit of Veronal that my doctor prescribes for me as a sleeping potion."

"But why?" Ginger asked.

"Alex is so much like my own son who succumbed to influenza after the war. My Alfie was such a good boy, taken from me far too soon. The difference between the two young men is obvious—the guidance of a good mother. I have no idea where his own mother is but she has obviously failed him. I just know that if I could just sit with him for a few days, just to talk…just to make him realise that he has someone here in London who can guide him." She sighed heavily and wrung pale, vein-covered hands. "My letters weren't working, so I concluded that the only way forward was to confront him in person and force him to listen. It was a simple thing to bribe the outgoing manager last year to keep some furnishings in the abandoned room and to secretly give me a key. He was leaving anyway to start his own hotel in Bristol."

She has been planning this for a long time, Ginger thought.

"You must admit it is a good plan," Mrs. Farnhurst said finally. "My only mistake was waiting too long to check on him, but I didn't think the drug would wear off so soon."

"It is most certainly not," Basil said, his voice rising slightly, "Not only is kidnapping highly illegal, it is also dangerous. You could have accidentally killed him by keeping him drugged while you employed your *motherly* advices. As it is, he did suffer a minor injury while scaling down that dilapidated drainpipe."

The only response from Mrs. Farnhurst was a slight tightening of her thin mouth as if she had just come upon some highly offensive odour.

"I'm afraid I have to place you under arrest for the kidnapping of Alex Simpson," Basil said. "We will afford you a few moments to get some things together and bring a bag."

"Oh, don't be silly, Mr. Reed. I've had a bag packed since the day I discovered that Alex had escaped. I knew it was only a matter of time before he went to the police. I actually thought you would be here sooner."

What cheek! Ginger held her tongue, deciding it was prudent not to mention that Mr. Simpson's memory lapse was the reason it had taken this long to find Mrs. Farnhurst.

"What are you waiting for, Chief Inspector?" Mrs. Farnhurst stood and stared impatiently. "Let's get on with it, then."

10

_T_HREE MONTHS LATER

THE CURTAIN CLOSED to enthusiastic cheers in the private screening room of Clapham Studios. This was the first full showing of the film _The Untold War_ and most of the producers, directors, actors, and production crew were in attendance. Along the far wall of the huge room were tables with trays of food and drinks of all kinds, including champagne. People began to leave their seats and move towards the tables while talking excitedly.

"It was so good of you to invite us all," Ginger said as she, Basil, and Felicia stood to greet Alex Simpson.

"On the contrary," the actor said, smiling and looking confident. "It was the least I could do, considering everything you have done for me." He cheerfully shook each of them by the hand, giving Felicia an extra moment and a wink. "Please let's sit down and have a chat." They settled into a row of velvet-upholstered seats. "Well, out with it. What did you think of the film?"

"Frightfully brilliant," Felicia gushed. "You were simply dashing in that role."

"I try to remain dashing at all times, Miss Gold, even while climbing down drainpipes in the rain."

"A wonderful film," Basil said. "Of course it is a bit disconcerting to relive that time, but on the other hand, it is important to remind ourselves and to think that hopefully we'll never go to war again."

Ginger agreed. "Very well done." In reality, she'd been rather shaken by the film and had shed tears during certain parts. But in the end she concluded that this, indeed, was something that a good story should be able to do—have an impact on both the mind and the soul. Besides, it was nice to have Basil put his arm around her for comfort.

Keeping her focus on Mr. Simpson, she asked pointedly, "How *are* you?"

"Do you mean, have I had any more *fugue* incidents? No, thank goodness. I honestly think that the process of reliving where I was and what I did during those moments of lost memory has somehow jarred my mind into sharp focus, and I do believe, thanks to you and Miss Gold, that I won't have to go through that again."

"Do you know now what caused the last one?" Felicia asked.

"I think so. The last scene that we had filmed before I wandered away was the moment where I witnessed a man being killed by a German hand grenade. Well… apparently that was a bit too close to reality. In 1916 near Verdun, I watched a good friend die in the same manner." He stared off into the distance and then shuddered. "Well, on a much brighter note, I want to introduce you to someone." He stood and called out to an attractive lady who'd been standing near a food table chatting with several people.

"Emily? Emily, can you please come and meet someone?" The beautiful lady revealed a dazzling smile as she walked over to them. "I want you to meet my fiancée, Miss Emily Lemaire."

Ginger glanced over at Felicia who returned her gaze with a look of mild resignation. Good for you, thought Ginger. She was hoping that Felicia had not pinned too much expectation on a relationship with Mr. Simpson. It seemed that Felicia was not overly heartbroken over this new development.

"How do you do," the fiancée said.

"Emily is an American actress," Mr. Simpson said. "We've

been seeing each other for a few months now. After this—episode—I decided I mustn't wait any longer."

"Alex has told me so much about you, and how you've helped him. I thank you too."

Hmm. Perhaps even poor Mrs. Farnhurst would approve of this one, Ginger thought.

As if reading her mind, Mr. Simpson said, "My mother... that is my *real* mother, has given her full blessing." He kissed Miss Lemaire on the cheek. "In fact, so has my sister and any other living relative that I have on this earth. Not to mention every friend I have ever had, including every bloke who occasionally shared a pint with me and survived to talk about it." They all laughed at this statement.

"When it's right... it's very right," Felicia said wistfully.

Ginger gave Felicia an affectionate hug. "This calls for champagne."

They walked over to one of the tables and they all took a glass. Ginger raised hers. "A toast," she said as they all lifted their glasses. "To time lost and regained, to memories worth remembering, and most importantly, to true love that does not seek to imprison, but rather to set us all free."

THE CASE OF THE
UNLUCKY CRICKETER

1

$\mathcal{T}$he cricket match was *Kent* versus *Middlesex*. Mrs. Ginger Reed, the former Lady Gold, was in attendance for the first time, and was quick to admit that the rules perplexed her. Baseball was the game she knew—having come of age in Boston—and she had many warm memories of long summer days spent at Fenway Park.

However, she'd heard so much about the famous *Lord's Cricket Ground*—one could hardly read a newspaper without encountering an article about Britain's beloved sport—and when her husband, Chief Inspector Basil Reed got his hands on two tickets, she was eager to accompany him.

Basil nudged her with restrained excitement. "Here he comes.."

Neville Sutcliffe, Basil's favourite player and one of the stars of the Middlesex team, approached the pitch with slow, easy strides.

The batsman, very tall and slender and dressed in the traditional whites, exited the pavilion carrying a bat and wearing pads on his legs.

Basil tipped his hat against the brightness of the sun, a rare treat after a string of damp days.

"The writers of various cricket magazines call him a graceful giraffe," he said with an amused grin. '*Unhurried and powerful*

51

with large prehensile hands that can catch anything, and bowl a ball with dynamic topspin'."

Ginger giggled. "Do they really use the word 'prehensile'?"

The skin around Basil's hazel eyes had sprouted crow's-feet and the hair around his temples was starting to grey. Ginger found this attractive, dignified, and undeniably debonair.

"At least one did," Basil answered. "I've been following Mr. Sutcliffe's career for a few years now. He is known as one of the best all-rounders in England."

Ginger, tucking a flyaway strand of her red bobbed hair under her felt cloche, raised a brow at yet another cricket term she'd never heard of before.

Basil immediately understood. "All-rounders can play well in the roles of both *batsman*—the player who hits the ball with a bat—and the *bowler*, the player who bowls the ball.

Ginger followed Basil's gaze and regarded Neville Sutcliffe as he took his position on the field. Basil continued to educate her.

"They call him 'The King of the Crease' because of how he tends to dominate the front of the wicket, preventing the bowler from getting that red leather ball past him and into the wicket."

The crowd grew quiet with anticipation.

The bowler made his approach, swinging his arms like a windmill, and then, using his entire body like a catapult, he hurled the ball towards the opposite wicket. Neville Sutcliffe waited with the flat of his bat poised in front of him, almost vertical with the tip resting on the ground. Ginger found the technique most intriguing. The ball bounced once and Mr. Sutcliffe manoeuvred the bat to defend the wicket. The ball appeared to be on a path to miss the wicket altogether due to a bit of a wild delivery. It clipped the very edge of the bat which redirected the trajectory towards the wicket, which was knocked completely asunder.

The crowd erupted with gasps of shock.

Basil, in an uncharacteristic display, yelled, "Bloody hell!" Which was followed by a glance of regret directed Ginger's way. "Awfully sorry, love, but that was most peculiar. Neville Sutcliffe just never, ever gets bowled out like that." He shook his head and stared at the pitch in bewilderment. "I've never known him be out for a *'golden duck'* before."

"Another odd term," Ginger said.

"Erm, yes. Unlike in baseball, in cricket the batsman can be dismissed by the very first ball that he faces. For some reason they call that a golden duck. I think due to the egg shape of the zero on the scoreboard."

Suddenly, another roar from the crowd rose up as Neville Sutcliffe angrily threw down his bat, stamped on it with his left foot, hastily tore off his leg pads, and stormed off the field. His team gawked after him as he disappeared into the team dressing room.

Basil pinched his lips in disapproval. "I say, what is the good fellow doing?"

"I think he has quit the game," Ginger said. It appeared that the outstanding Mr. Sutcliffe could use a lesson in sportsmanship.

"This is very unusual for him. One doesn't get this far in one's career by behaving in such an ungentlemanly manner. Something must be amiss."

After a long delay, play was eventually resumed, but Ginger noted that Basil's enthusiasm had waned considerably.

"Ginger, darling, would you mind if we left?" he asked after a short while. "I fear I have lost my stomach for this match."

"Not at all," Ginger said. She collected her handbag and arranged the strap over the shoulder of her new Jean Lavin fine-knit cardigan.

They'd just reached Ginger's 1924 cream and red Crossley Sports Tourer, which was parked in the large parking area beside the grounds, when a man's voice reached them from behind.

"Hello there! Would you mind holding on for just a moment?"

Ginger kept her surprise in check when they pivoted towards Neville Sutcliffe, now dressed in a brown tweed blazer, V-neck sweater, and straw boater. The long-legged man strode smoothly their way with an earnest look on his face. "Sir? Am I correct in presuming that you are Mr. Basil Reed of Scotland Yard? One of my teammates said he thought he recognised you."

Basil caught Ginger's gaze before answering. "How can I help you, Mr. Sutcliffe?"

"I do beg your pardon, but it's your wife that I am hoping to speak to." His blue eyes bore into Ginger. "You must be Mrs. Reed, otherwise known as Lady Gold of Lady Gold Investigations." He offered his hand to Ginger and she extended her gloved one. "I am."

"I'm so pleased to meet you. You see, I'm rather hoping you'll be open to a new case."

Ginger and Basil shared a surprised look. "That depends, Mr. Sutcliffe. What is it that you need investigating?"

"It's a frightfully odd situation, but I just can't go on this way."

"What way is that?" Basil asked.

"Fouling up in my cricket matches. I really do need your help. Someone has stolen my lucky bat."

2
____

*G*inger wasn't the superstitious type, but she was aware that it was a trait common to those who followed sporting events. "Your lucky bat?"

Mr. Sutcliffe's long forehead buckled in consternation. "I know it sounds foolish, but I swear by it, and now," he flapped his long arms, "the results of this theft are plain for everyone to see." He took off his hat to reveal medium-length sandy-blond hair. "My apologies for that childish display you just witnessed on the pitch."

Ginger guessed the cricketer was in his late twenties. Not film-star handsome, but his complexion was clear, and frequent exposure to the sun brought out freckles on his long nose. The corners of his wide mouth were turned downwards.

"I'm afraid I can't continue playing until the matter is resolved. I know that it was uncouth of me to leave the match abruptly like that, but without my bat, I'm just no good whatsoever to the team. I can't seem to bat properly, or bowl, or field. I don't care if they fire me, I won't step back onto that pitch until I get it back." He looked at Ginger imploringly. "Will you help me?"

"A chief inspector from Scotland Yard is standing before you now," Ginger said. "Why is it that you would not go to the police first?"

Neville Sutcliffe looked at Basil questioningly. "Well, I don't know that the police would have time for such a seemingly trivial matter."

Basil agreed. "I'm afraid that might be true."

"Of course," Mr. Sutcliffe went on, "to me it is far from trivial. This particular bat has been with me since I was a youngster. Its importance to me reaches far beyond sentimental value and I do believe it brings me luck, even when I'm not using it in a match. Simply knowing it's in my dressing room does the trick. I maintain it religiously, and only use it for important matches, thus it has outlasted any other cricket bats of its kind. In fact, it was given to me by my grandfather, who was himself a well-known cricket player in his time. On the rare occasions that I have forgotten it while playing away, my performance, particularly in front of the wicket, has been deplorable, just like it was today. I hope you understand the reason for my consternation."

The matter was rather intriguing, Ginger admitted, she wasn't in need of another case particularly, but Neville Sutcliffe meant something to Basil, and for that reason alone she found herself nodding her head.

"I have an office on Regent Street," she said. Offering him her card, she added, "If you ring my assistant, Miss Gold, she'll arrange an appointment for you to come to discuss the details with us."

EARLY IN THE afternoon the next day, Ginger sat across the desk from Mr. Sutcliffe in the office of Lady Gold Investigations to discuss the case. Boss, Ginger's Boston terrier—a gift from her father soon after the great war, in which her first husband, Daniel, had died—lay ensconced in his favourite spot in a basket at Ginger's feet. As usual, he was fast asleep and emitted the occasional soft snore. Her former sister-in-law, Felicia Gold, was a published mystery writer, who found the quiet atmosphere at the office more conducive to creative productivity than the busyness of life at Hartigan House, where they both lived. From her position at her desk, which ran adjacent to Ginger's and just behind the client chairs, she took in the young man, a rare sighting since the war, with a look of flirtatious interest. Ginger cleared her throat with a pointed look, and Felicia quickly picked up her pencil and notepad, giving Ginger a glance of faux contriteness.

"Now then," Ginger started, "when did you last see your lucky bat?"

Mr. Sutcliffe stretched out his long legs. "Three days ago, at the beginning of the match at Lord's. It may seem frivolous, but I've paid for some special lockable storage. I supply my own combination lock. I'd put my bat in the compartment at the beginning of the match, with the intention of bringing it out should the need arise."

"What kind of need, Mr. Sutcliffe?" Felicia asked.

Neville Sutcliffe turned his long neck and smiled with appreciation at Felicia's exposed calves.

"If my team were to lose too many wickets, for example, Miss Gold." Reverting his attention to Ginger, he continued, "Much to my consternation, I performed very poorly on my first time batting. In the middle of the match, I began to suspect something nefarious must've happened to my bat, as dramatic as that might sound. However, I never imagined that someone would actually steal it. Shortly thereafter I was able to check." He paused for effect. "My suspicions were confirmed. The combination lock was smashed and the door had been left wide open."

"That must've been quite a shock," Ginger said.

"Yes, quite," Mr. Sutcliffe said stiffly. "Damnable behaviour by some scallywag set on undermining my good record by nicking my bat!"

Felicia paused with her pencil hovering in mid-air. "How unusual that you started playing poorly without even knowing that your bat was gone."

Mr. Sutcliffe shifted his chair and faced Felicia. "It is, isn't it? Furthermore, it's proof that the bat has some sort of connection to me."

"Was anyone with you when you discovered the bat was missing?" Ginger asked.

"No, I was alone. The rest of the players were out sitting on the pavilion balcony."

Ginger leaned back in her chair. "I'm assuming you've asked your team members about it."

"Oh yes, I asked everyone including the manager, Mr. Adamson. No one had any idea of what had happened to my lucky bat, of course. I highly doubt it was anyone on the team, anyway. There's the legendary loyalty that exists in county cricket teams. Most members, like me, grew up in the county they're playing for. We've known each other since we were children—like brothers. It's unthinkable that any player would do anything to risk the team in any way."

"How many people knew that you had a lucky bat?" Ginger asked. "Was it common knowledge?"

"That's hard to say. I don't talk about it at all, but something like that is impossible to keep secret for any amount of time, at least from my team members. It's quite obvious when we are travelling by rail or by car to an away match that I have the bat with me. So, to answer your question, I suppose anyone could know if they were curious enough to ask about it."

"Every crime has a motive, Mr. Sutcliffe," Ginger said. "Why would someone want to steal your lucky bat?"

"I suppose it could have been anyone on the opposing team." He pulled in his legs, his pointy knees jutting upwards. "Maybe that's where you should start?"

Ginger didn't relish the task of interviewing the entire Kent team and its management to find a missing lucky bat.

"Unless it was a total stranger." Mr. Sutcliffe's expression brightened with the dawning of a new idea. "A deranged lunatic! A crazed fan, perhaps. I'm quite well known, you know," he added cheekily. "Some say I'm famous."

"*C*an you think of anyone who specifically has a grudge against you, Mr. Sutcliffe?" Ginger asked. "On either team?"

The cricketer pinched his lips and blew them out again. "Someone who wants me to play poorly, and for my team to lose, I suppose. That could be anyone. In fact, Middlesex did end up losing against Kent yesterday, by a hundred and fifty runs." He grunted. "A terrible defeat. I am loath to face my teammates at our next match." His chin fell to his chest. "I need to get my bat back."

"Do you live alone?" Ginger asked.

"Yes. I have a flat near Hyde Park. I did have a flatmate for a while, Mr. Kabir Patil, but he wanted to be on his own and left."

Ginger felt quite certain there was more to that story and made a mental note to speak to Mr. Patil.

"Can you please describe your bat?" she asked.

"It's made out of English willow, though the colour of it has turned to an almost chestnut-brown due to being oiled so often. The Gunn & Moore company of Nottingham made it and the trademark is stamped on it, although it is quite faded now. There are nicks on it from hundreds of balls, of course. Besides its age, the thing that would distinguish it is that there are words burned onto the back of it: *To my grandson Neville, signed Alan 'The Cannon' Sutcliffe.* My grandfather's nickname."

Boss stood up in his basket to stretch and Ginger reached down to pat his head. "We will try to help you, Mr. Sutcliffe," she said finally as she straightened back up in her chair. "I do have some reservations about the case, but Miss Gold and I will do our best and see what comes of it."

"Thank you so very much, Mrs. Reed. I know it's a bit of an odd case, but your reputation has begun to precede you, and I am hopeful we will have a good outcome."

"Reputation can be like a pendulum," Ginger said as she rose to shake his hand. "Sometimes it swings the wrong way."

MIDDLESEX MANAGER MR. JOHN ADAMSON worked in an office in the pavilion of Lord's Cricket Ground. It was an austere but comfortable office that had a large wooden desk with an office chair and two small wicker chairs for guests where Ginger and Felicia where presently seated. Boss lay on the carpeted floor chewing on a dog toy that Ginger had brought along.

"My wife and I have a beagle. We call him *Sergeant*," Mr. Adamson said gruffly as he regarded Boss when they had first walked into the office. "I am quite fond of the dodgy little beggar although he eats more than you would think for such a little grounder."

The room had a large window that looked out onto the pitch, and various mounted pictures on the wall showed the cricket team of Middlesex through all its iterations over the last twenty or more years. Mr. Adamson was a fit-looking middle-aged man with shortly cropped grey hair and grey eyes. His skin had a sun-browned and weathered look, undoubtedly from many hours outdoors. His no-nonsense demeanour immediately reminded Ginger of someone who might have been an officer in the military. Indeed, after they had sat down, she noticed a picture of a younger version of the man posing in a sergeant major's uniform.

"I was a bit surprised when you called," he said as he folded a newspaper and pushed it aside. "And then of course, I read this." He slid a sports news magazine towards Ginger and turned it so she could read the cover. *The Cricketer's Voice.*

The headline in question read: *Middlesex Player's Lucky Bat Stolen–Enlists Services of Private Detective.* Ginger picked up the magazine and perused the story. It contained a brief account of Mr. Sutcliffe's exit from the field during the anticipated match, and the subsequent employing of Lady Gold Investigations. Lean on specific details, the article focused more on Mr. Sutcliffe's performance statistics and a commentary on Middlesex's standing in the season so far. The entire piece was short and vague, however, Ginger was aghast to see her name printed in a sports magazine without her prior knowledge.

"My secretary dropped this onto my desk this morning," Mr. Adamson said as he watched Ginger's reaction. "It was just published yesterday."

"I am not pleased with this, Mr. Adamson. How did this get into the press?" She handed the article to Felicia to read.

"Well, I was hoping you could tell me, but I see from your response that you are as surprised as I am."

"Yes, I am. I can't imagine Mr. Sutcliffe doing it. What would he have to gain by it?"

"I agree." Mr. Adamson sniffed. "It's not really the type of thing that a top player would necessarily want printed in the press. So far this is the only publication carrying it. But the day is still young."

"I suppose that cat is out of the bag now," Ginger said resolutely.

Felicia once again took out her notebook. "What are your thoughts on this missing bat?"

Mr. Adamson scratched his ear. "I don't really know what to think. Although I take no stock in such superstitious rubbish, it is common for many players to do so. You would be surprised at how many of them have good luck charms or routines that they go through every day to bring them luck. But definitely, our last match was heavily influenced by the poor performance of our star player." Sniffing again, he added, "It was rather unsports-manlike of him to leave the field for the rest of the match. I thought he had gone mad! Something like that affects the whole team's performance in a match. I am all for getting that bat back if it means we can have him in top form again. I'd have petitioned to throw him off the team already if it weren't for the fact that he is one of our top assets."

"Who had access to that dressing room during the match?" Ginger asked.

"The dressing rooms are not open to the public," Mr. Adamson replied. "The only access during a match is from the pavilion, which is open to players from both teams during matches as well as retired Middlesex players. All outside doors are locked to those rooms. I have questioned the general staff here at Lord's and you, of course, are welcome to do the same. However, I sincerely doubt you'll get anywhere with that. I know everyone who works here. I can't imagine anyone stealing a bloody bat from a sodding dressing room!"

"Who do you think might have a motive?" Ginger asked. "So far we have not really been able to isolate a clear reason for the theft other than the obvious, which would be someone from the opposing team or someone employed by them."

Mr. Adamson snatched a handkerchief from his pocket and dabbed at his nose. "I really don't think that's what happened. I know the manager of the Kent team very well, Mr. Clive Holland. He's a tough bloke, and a hard man to get on with. I guess a little bit like me." His chuckle was like sandpaper on wood. "Until you get to know him that is. His players all respect him well enough." He paused for a moment, gazing out through the window over the pitch. "Our daughter was very ill a few years ago with very powerful influenza. We almost lost her. He sent cards and flowers every week to her hospital room, and his wife cooked casseroles and had them delivered to us. He is a devout, religious man who doesn't even use foul language or drink alcohol. I just cannot imagine he would sanction an underhanded trick like stealing a lucky bat from a locked dressing room."

With scrunched eyebrows, he returned his gaze to Ginger. "He can be a disagreeable old codger, and *he is* the manager of one of our biggest rival teams, but he is also a man of principle. I honestly think he would immediately fire any man on his team who would do something like this."

Ginger let out a short breath of frustration. Finding an entry point in this case was proving difficult indeed.

"I do have a suspicion..." Mr. Adamson added hesitantly. "I am not one to gossip..."

"Go on please, Mr. Adamson," Ginger prompted. "At this point I am open to hearing any theory you may have."

"Well you see, there is the rather awkward point about Neville Sutcliffe's father, Oscar Sutcliffe." He looked at them both as if wondering if he should say more, then with a rather resolute sniff, pressed on with a note of sarcasm. "I gather Sutcliffe failed to mention that part of the bat's history. Yes, you see the bat originally belonged to Mr. Alan Sutcliffe. Otherwise known as '*The Cannon*' by cricket enthusiasts. Alan Sutcliffe was Neville's grandfather and a player of some distinction many years ago for Middlesex. However, Oscar Sutcliffe, Neville's father, was also, for a brief time, a cricketer for Middlesex. The two elder Sutcliffes had a great falling out just as Oscar's career was starting to gain momentum for the team. I don't know what the issue was for sure, but the result was that Alan Sutcliffe's famous lucky bat, which had been passed down to Oscar, was taken back, actually *it was stolen back,* right here in the dressing room at Lord's by his father—Neville's grandfather—Alan. Can you imagine such a thing?"

Mr. Adamson threw up his hands, his handkerchief still firmly in his fist, waving as a flag of surrender. "Anyway, shortly thereafter Oscar suffered an injury to his left leg in a bizarre cycling accident. That marked not only the end of his career as a cricket player, but any civil relationship between Oscar and Alan. The two became estranged and remain so to this day."

Felicia lowered her pencil. "A frightfully sad story!"

"Yes, I suppose it is, Miss Gold."

"Our client hasn't mentioned any of this," Ginger said, feeling rather annoyed by the fact. "What of Neville's mother?"

"Died a few years ago from what I understand," Mr. Adamson replied. "The same influenza that almost got my daughter, and word has it that Alan Sutcliffe is now ailing terribly."

Mr. Adamson leaned forward, planted his elbows on his knees, and stared at Ginger. "But here's the interesting thing: Neville and his father, Oscar, are also on bad terms; and so, Mrs. Reed, if I were you, I would be asking myself this: Is history repeating itself here in an ironic twist?"

4

A fter Mr. Adamson's rather astounding insinuation, Ginger and Felicia made immediate plans to interview Mr. Oscar Sutcliffe, who, fortunately, agreed to meet them in a small cafe not far from Ginger's office.

Oscar Sutcliffe was a tall, slim middle-aged man with deep-set blue eyes and light complexion. Unlike his son, he wore a moustache, and his thinning sandy-blond hair was greying at the temples. He walked with a cane and had a slight limp, favouring his left leg. Dressed casually in a cardigan, he took the third chair at the small table and sat.

After an amused glance at Boss, who sat dutifully at Ginger's feet, he got abruptly to the point. "I came to clear any suspicion that I might have something to do with my son's missing bat. I read about the whole ridiculous affair in a sports magazine earlier today." His tone was dismissive, and his stiff posture spoke of impatience and annoyance. "I am a little surprised that he even told you about me. We rarely talk," he indicated his left leg, "and I rather think he is embarrassed by his father."

The waitress approached and tea was ordered.

Ginger returned her attention to Mr. Oscar Sutcliffe. "Actually, your son didn't mention you at all. I find the omission puzzling. I would think the history of the bat would be important to mention."

The elder Sutcliffe harrumphed.

"We were given your name by another party who thought it might be worthwhile to contact you." Ginger didn't want to divulge how they knew about him, hoping to avoid spreading any more animosity than there already was between the characters in this sad story.

Oscar Sutcliffe wasn't fooled. "You mean someone thinks that I stole it! I—"

The tea arrived and Mr. Sutcliffe's outburst was thwarted. Ginger slipped Boss a piece of the accompanying biscuit, while keeping her eye on Mr. Sutcliffe. She took her first sip, giving Felicia a subtle glance for her to remain silent and wait for their guest to continue speaking.

Their patience was rewarded, as Mr. Sutcliffe picked up the conversation again. Apparently, a bit of tea calmed his nerves, as he sounded rather more reasonable when he continued. "Well, I guess I can't blame a person for questioning my integrity. It would definitely hold some irony had I actually taken it."

"We've heard the story about you and your father," Ginger admitted.

Oscar Sutcliffe harrumphed again. "There is no end to my father's selfishness. I would tell you to go and investigate *him* in this so-called crime except that he is on his deathbed from what I hear. Maybe he paid someone to do it, just to make me look bad. I wouldn't put it past the old blighter."

"But, why would he steal the bat from his own grandson?" Felicia asked.

"Why would he steal it from his own son?" Mr. Sutcliffe demanded loudly. His eyes darted around the cafe and he lowered his voice. "He's a bitter, self-serving old man who expects perfection from everyone. No wonder my mother was driven to an early grave. People called him *'The Cannon'*." He chuckled bitterly. "Well, that *Cannon* was even better at hurling invectives than cricket balls. No one escaped his scrutiny or his scathing rebuke. He stole the bat from me because he was impatient with my playing. I had a few rough matches and suddenly the bat was gone! Of course, I suspected him but had no proof.

My suspicions were confirmed when I found out that he had, years later, given the bat to Neville."

"I am very sorry for asking this," Ginger started with reluctance, "but it could be very pertinent to this investigation. Is that why the relationship is strained between you and your son? Because Alan Sutcliffe gave him the bat?"

Oscar Sutcliffe lifted a thin shoulder. "Neville was always much closer to his mother than I was, and I think that when she died we just drifted apart. He may resemble me in appearance, but in personality, he is far more like his mother's side of the family. Our marriage was a troubled one, and Neville resented me, as if I was somehow to blame for her illness. I won't bore you with more detail than that, even though like most women, you are probably eager for the gossip."

Ginger kept her expression blank at the rude remark, though she saw Felicia's mouth drop slightly open. She shot her sister-in-law a look to keep her from speaking her mind at this moment. It wouldn't do to rebuke the man now and still hope to get any useful information out of him.

Mr. Sutcliffe didn't seem to notice and continued. "So to answer your question... yes, Neville's bat is a reminder of my father's rejection of me. Whoever stole the bat did me a favour. I hope the bat is never found and that Alan Sutcliffe dies without seeing his grandson win another match for Middlesex. If I'm honest, I will say that it makes me glad to imagine him on his deathbed, wrinkled and frail."

Ginger blinked back the shock she felt at the older man's vitriol. She had some experience with family tensions and even with overbearing elders. Ambrosia, her grandmother-in-law through her deceased first husband, Daniel Gold, came to her mind. However, Ambrosia seemed almost agreeable compared to members of the Sutcliffe family tree.

Oscar Sutcliffe gripped his cane and started to rise, indicating he had had enough of this conversation.

"Do you think the bat actually brings luck?" Felicia asked.

Mr. Sutcliffe straightened his shoulders while leaning on his cane. "You tell me, Miss Gold. I played like a champion when I had it. As soon as it was taken from me, not only did my playing suffer greatly, so did I." He tapped his left leg. "The injury to my leg happened when I was hit by a lorry while I was on my bicycle. The street was practically deserted and yet the driver managed to run me down. He claimed he didn't see me! The accident happened only three days after my father stole my bat from me. I am thoroughly convinced that in doing so he stole my good career and my good health. I am reminded of it every time I have to endure the pain of taking a step. Yes, the bat is lucky but it is a vindictive, clinging type of luck that is loath to let go of a man. I wish I had never laid eyes upon the blasted thing. Now, if you'll excuse me, and even if you won't—I have an important matter to attend to." Without waiting for an answer or extending a proper goodbye, he hobbled out of the cafe.

Felicia stared at the man through the window as he limped across the street. "What cheek!"

Ginger gathered her things, along with Boss' leash, and motioned for Felicia to do the same.

"Where are we going?" Felicia said, reaching for her handbag.

"That man annoys me, and just for that, we are going to follow him to see what his 'important' matter is."

They rushed out of the café, down the street to where Ginger had the Crossley parked. Due to many experiences not only in the war where she had served as a spy for British intelligence, but also in the course of many criminal investigations, Ginger knew how to follow someone without detection. She kept her eye on Oscar Sutcliffe as he struggled with his cane and climbed into his own motorcar, a black two-seater Bentley sports tourer.

Ginger started the engine.

"Tally-ho!" Felicia said while holding on to her hat. It was a manoeuvre she had quickly learned to adopt in her many driving expeditions with Ginger, especially on warm days like today when the Crossley's top was folded down.

Boss jumped onto the seat between them, and Felicia pulled him onto her lap. "C'mon, Boss. I think you and I are due for some thrills, eh?"

Ginger smiled and engaged the gear lever. The car lurched forward.

$\mathcal{M}$uch to Ginger's enjoyment, Oscar Sutcliffe was also someone who liked to drive at higher speeds, perhaps a subconscious attempt to make up for his lack of motion on foot. Following him through the streets of London was a bit of a boisterous adventure. He led them north initially and then around Regents Park, and at times it felt rather more like a chase than a simple follow. Ginger almost lost him several times due to heavy traffic, however, by clever use of side streets and alleyways, she was able to reacquire the quarry.

As she swerved mightily to avoid hitting a large delivery lorry, the driver sounded his horn and waved his fist. Ginger was thankful that the Crossley was an agile machine and up to the task. She forced the gear lever through the gears and feathered the brakes with precision.

A sharp turn required Ginger to sound her horn to warn a bicyclist out of the way. Felicia gripped both her hat and Boss tightly. A slow-moving double-decker bus required Ginger to accelerate quickly to overtake it, which forced her to jerk the Crossley in order to miss crashing into another motorcar. Boss let out an excited yelp.

London drivers are much too sedate, Ginger thought for the hundredth time.

Oscar Sutcliffe eventually turned into Roberts Avenue in the

Camden area. He slowed as he turned into a long driveway in front of very large red-brick Edwardian house set on large plot of land. The immaculately painted house had beautifully ornate bay window frames and carved balcony railings. It was one of the largest houses Ginger had seen in this part of London, rivalling Hartigan House in size.

Ginger slowly drove past the driveway, careful to time it exactly right so that Mr. Sutcliffe wouldn't spot them. At the end of the road she turned the Crossley around and parked. It appeared that Mr. Sutcliffe wasn't the only one with business at the big house. They witnessed several more cars driving up to the same address.

Was something going on in that house? Perhaps a party or some kind of meeting. Ginger noticed that all the drivers were middle-aged or older men with no females amongst them. Most of the cars were expensive make—Bentleys, Vauxhalls, Alfa Romeos, and even a Jaguar had turned in. Oscar Sutcliffe kept affluent company, apparently.

"Not exactly a flapper event, I'll wager," Felicia joked.

"No. More like some kind of old boys club."

Ginger noted the time and turned the car back around towards South Kensington. She would need Basil's help with this part of the puzzle. She glanced at Felicia. "Did you happen to notice any phone boxes on the way here?"

"I think so," Felicia said, "Just down a little way. Why do you ask?"

"I need to ring Scotland Yard. Basil should still be there at this time of day." Ginger had a hunch and she wanted her husband's opinion.

After a few moments, she found the distinctive red and white phone box on the corner of intersecting streets. She mused inwardly as she climbed out of the Crossley about how wonderful it would be if someday, someone could invent a phone that she could take with her in the car.

"I'm terribly sorry to bother you at work," she said, once their call was connected, "but this is concerning the case involving Mr. Sutcliffe."

"No trouble at all, love. How is the investigation going and how can I help?"

"I'll fill you in on the details later, but for now I'm wondering if you happen to know anything about a particular house in Camden?"

After a pause, Basil said, "You surely don't mean number fourteen on Roberts Avenue?"

"Why yes, that's it! How did you know?"

"That house was under our surveillance for a time earlier this year. The owner is a Mr. John Fensworth. He's a well-known art collector, but we've suspected him of art *theft,* as well as the thievery of famous celebrity memorabilia and so forth. There are allegations that he sometimes holds both public and private showings that attract certain wealthy gentlemen from all over Europe, where he either sells items or simply displays them. We stopped the surveillance about a month ago though, because it was not producing any results and Mr. Fensworth was thought to have left London by rail on a long holiday. In any event, we never did observe any gatherings and we didn't have enough evidence for a legal search."

"Well, I think there is such a gathering going on at the house right now. Felicia and I are parked just down the street and have observed at least a dozen fine cars entering the property in the last twenty minutes."

"He must be back. By Jove, I need to get over there!"

"Are you going to bring officers with you and search the place?" Ginger asked.

"No, we can't do that just yet. I'll explain later."

"Well, if you do gain entrance to the house, can you please do something for me?"

"If I can. What is it?"

"Look for an old cricket bat that has the words *To my grandson Neville, signed Alan 'The Cannon' Sutcliffe* inscribed on the back of it."

"Good heavens," Basil said simply, and then rang off.

THE NEXT EVENING, Ginger and Basil snuggled together on the

settee in the sitting room, and as they often did after a long day's work, shared what they could over a glass of brandy. Pippins had ensured that the fire was lit, and Boss snored from his basket next to the hearth.

Ginger, wistful that she hadn't been able to join Basil on this tour through the mysterious house in Camden, was eager to hear how it went. "Do tell, love," she said with a playful poke. "I'm on pins and needles!"

Basil smiled coyly. "Righto. Where shall I begin?"

"Why not with how you managed to get in? I don't imagine you were on the guest list. Weren't you concerned you might be recognised from the Yard?"

"There's always that possibility for any of our inspectors," Basil admitted. "However, I think that most of the guests are from outside the city. Some of them may not even be English. It's true, I wasn't on the guest list, however, we had already set up a certain *alias* for me; that is, a false identity I was to use should there ever be a reason to gain entry to Roberts Avenue. According to false documentation, I am a certain Walter McDonald from Glasgow. Mr. McDonald is very wealthy and likes to dabble in stolen art. His name has been purposely peppered in certain art enthusiast magazines over the last year, and in some questionable publications that are known to be information conduits for the illegal art trade in Great Britain. This was done by a special secret task unit at Scotland Yard. I was certain Fensworth would be glad to receive the well-to-do Scotsman, invitation or not."

"Oh, do let me hear your Glaswegian accent!"

"Och lassie, you sound a wee bit surprised t' know of ma fine Scottish brogue," Basil said. Ginger laughed. Her husband sounded a lot like Will Fyffe, the famous Glaswegian comedic radio personality.

"Before I tell you what I found, please tell me how your investigation is going? What on earth were you doing there?"

Ginger relayed what she had found so far, including the interview with the manager and how he had led them to Oscar Sutcliffe.

"What a bizarre story," Basil shook his head in amazement. "I am sad to hear that the Sutcliffe family is so at odds."

"Indeed. So, what did you find?" Ginger's boldness in asking about a Scotland Yard case wasn't out of place. She and Basil had an understanding. They each had their own investigations and respected the need for confidentiality. They never expected one of them to divulge information to the other just for the sake of conversation. However, their cases often overlapped, and at times Basil made a special request that Ginger consult with Scotland Yard. In those instances they were cleared to be forthright and honest.

"I saw your man Oscar Sutcliffe last night," Basil said, "and spoke to him briefly. He's a rather boorish fellow all right, but appeared to have done quite well for himself as an art dealer. He built up enough of a name for himself in cricket to gain entrance into this gentlemen's club and the world of selling and collecting art and famous collectors' items.

"After a time, we were all shown several galleries of mostly paintings and film memorabilia. I recognised a famous vampire costume that was worn by Armando Falconi in an Italian motion picture. It's been missing for some time. Also, a diamond necklace stolen in France from *Hélène Darly*, the famous French actress. But the most important find last night was a stolen painting called *Tuscany Harvest* by Italian painter *Pietro di Gavisconetti*. It has been missing for over a year, and for *that* little discovery, Ginger, Scotland Yard is immensely grateful to you, and for you ringing me yesterday."

Basil sipped his brandy, then added, "Needless to say, Fensworth had an unwelcome visit from Scotland Yard late last night soon after I left."

"Oh mercy. Well I'm glad to be of help to the constabulary of course, and those articles are certainly important, but you haven't mentioned anything about a certain cricket bat."

Basil gazed at her apologetically. "I *did* actually ask Fensworth about it when I had a moment to pull him aside. He told me he would dearly love to have that bat and that it would no doubt fetch a tidy sum. But alas, all his sources, as nefarious and far-reaching as they may be, had no news of the bat or how it came to be missing."

Ginger sighed. She was quickly running out of viable ideas. She had no wish to interview the entire Kent team and its management, and was almost ready to give up pursuing this frustrating and sad case any further.

But, she did have one more idea.

6

———

The next day, following some advice given to her by Middlesex manager John Adamson, Ginger found Kabir Patil, Neville Sutcliffe's former flatmate, in a coffeehouse called *The Match* just a few minutes' walk from Lord's. It had a lunch menu that clearly catered to cricket players and enthusiasts, with sandwiches cleverly titled *Wicketkeepers Cheese and Pickle* and *Bowler's Beef and Mustard*. The rich and sweet scents of coffee and fresh bread met her as she entered the establishment.

Ginger had chosen a very business-like outfit: a grey and yellow two-piece suit with a pleated skirt in a tartan pattern, a matching yellow cloche hat with a grey band, and sensible black pumps. She wasn't sure how women entered this particular cafe and so she wanted to appear as if she were a member of the press and not attract undue attention.

This was part of the reason why she did not like her name or photos printed in the press in connection with her investigations, especially without her consent. Anonymity as a private detective was often key to her success. For this same reason she had decided to leave both Felicia and Boss at the office while she interviewed Mr. Patil. Her companions definitely drew attention.

Ginger had an increasing amount of disquiet about this case and was frustrated by her lack of progress. She wanted another perspective on the case, and hoped to gain it by interviewing someone else, who had not, by Neville Sutcliffe's own admission, got along with him that well.

The team manager had pointed out Mr. Patil in a group picture of the team, so she recognised him sitting at a table alone at the end of the room, eating a sandwich and drinking coffee. An earnest-looking man about the same age as Neville Sutcliffe, he had thick, short-cropped black hair, dark skin, and brown eyes.

"I was wondering how long it would take before you came looking for me," Mr. Patil said after she had introduced herself and asked if she could take the seat across from him.

"Oh?" Ginger looked at him in mild surprise as she sat down.

"Yes, I read the article in *The Cricketer's Voice*. I ordered a pot of tea," he said, nodding toward a teapot and two empty teacups. "I hope I wasn't too presumptuous."

"Not at all. I have a hankering for tea, as it so happens." Ginger removed her leather gloves and placed them on the table and then poured the tea for the two of them. "So, Mr. Patil, I gather you assumed I would be coming to see you at some point?"

Mr. Patil accepted his tea, pausing to blow on it. "Yes, I did, and that assumption was confirmed when Mr Adamson told me you might be dropping in here today. To be honest, I thought it would probably take a few days or even longer, but I knew you would eventually run out of any real leads in this case, and therefore that the path would end up at me. Any good investigator would have asked Sutcliffe about past relationships, colleagues, and so on. My name would have eventually come up in conversation with him or anyone else who knows him."

Ginger stared at her companion over her teacup. "That's all very perceptive of you." She sipped the tea and set the cup back into its saucer. "In that case, I certainly would like to hear your thoughts about the missing bat and about Neville Sutcliffe in general."

"Certainly," Mr. Patil said. "As you know, Mr. Sutcliffe and I shared a flat just near Hyde Park for about a year. He's an amiable fellow, both off the field and on. We got along well enough at first, but then it became an issue paying the rent." He shrugged. "I moved out over a month ago."

"Well, that is surprising," Ginger said. "I would think that a player of his calibre would get paid a good salary."

"He does get paid a good salary by Middlesex. More than most I would say. But when you are a man with an addiction..."

Ginger raised a brow, keeping her gaze locked on his.

Mr. Patil elaborated. "Gambling, Mrs Reed. Neville Sutcliffe has a severe gambling addiction."

Ginger felt the familiar sensation in her mind of jigsaw puzzle pieces starting to click together. Commercialised betting had been illegal in England for many years with the exception of horse racing. Corrupt lotteries and well-publicised fraud cases had brought on the passing of anti-gambling legislation. However, unregulated betting practices and gambling house activities were still rampant, and gambling syndicates that engaged in extortion and illegal moneylending were very hard to prosecute.

Mr. Patil continued, "Neville couldn't pay his half of the rent. This went on for two months, and he refused to give me a clear answer as to why, though he did become more distressed as time went on. He could be very short-tempered. He stopped sleeping and started drinking. Unbelievably though, this didn't affect his cricket playing. It was as if lady luck was sitting on his shoulder on the field, even when he had a hangover. Too bad she didn't like accompanying him to the card table as well. One night he came home drunk as a lord. I'd had enough at this point and we had a huge row. He finally admitted that he had a gambling problem and that he owed certain unsavoury characters a lot of money. He said he was engaging in cards mostly, but also horses, greyhound racing..."

He paused and drew a breath. "Sports betting, Mrs. Reed. I suspect he might've even started betting on cricket matches."

"Oh mercy."

Mr. Patil sipped his tea, his gaze darting furtively around the cafe. "I moved out the next day and kept my mouth shut."

"Thank you for this information," Ginger said. The puzzle pieces were most definitely clicking into place.

Mr. Patil leaned in. "He lives alone now, so he must have

found a way to make full rent payments. I can't imagine how and I don't want to know."

Looking put out, the young man worked his lips before adding, "I don't want any part of this, but if I were you, Mrs. Reed, and I were looking for that bat..." He pulled out a key, placed it on the table, and slid it over to Ginger. "This is a spare. My name is still on the rental agreement." He paused, as he held her gaze. "I think I left a jar of *brilliantine* there. I wonder if it's not too much trouble for you to collect it for me?"

Ginger nodded slowly, understanding his meaning.

"Neville's not usually at home at this time of day. The flat will take you ten minutes to get to by motorcar."

Mr. Patil said his goodbyes as he pushed away from the table. Ginger pocketed the key.

7

_____

*G*inger slid Mr. Patil's spare key into the solid wooden door of flat number twenty-nine on the second floor of the Victorian-style building in Paddington. The door opened noiselessly, and she entered the spacious flat and looked around. It was very tastefully decorated with what looked like a new kitchen and modern furniture. Part of her training for her duties in the Great War had included how to search a room systematically and thoroughly without wasting time. She moved confidently and quickly across the sitting room and went directly to the room in obvious use by Neville Sutcliffe. The pictures on the wall hung slightly askew and there were tangled sheets on an unmade bed. Dirty clothes were piled both on the floor and on top of the mirrored dressing table. The door of the wardrobe was left open and Ginger spread apart the clothes hanging from the rail. Leaning against the back wall was a well-worn chestnut-coloured cricket bat with the trademark of *Gunn & Moore* emblazoned on it.

Ginger hummed. Not a very inventive hiding spot.

She picked up the bat and examined it for the inscription and found it easily. Just as she crossed the threshold of the bedroom and headed for the exit, she heard a man's voice say, "Not so fast!"

In a split second, the bat was forcibly wrenched out of her

grasp. Ginger gasped and turned to face Neville Sutcliffe. She suddenly regretted leaving Boss at Hartigan House. Her pet would surely have heard him come into the flat and warned her. Like a ticker tape, comments that the press had written flashed across her mind: *as graceful as a giraffe; unhurried and powerful with large prehensile hands that can catch anything.*

Middlesex's star player had certainly moved quickly and quietly in order for Ginger to miss hearing him enter the flat.

The look on Neville Sutcliffe's face was a mixture of pain, bewilderment, and anger. "I thought you worked for me?"

"I do," Ginger said calmly. "And my investigation led me here. You shouldn't be at all surprised."

He let out a tight laugh. "I guess I didn't fully believe all the things that I had heard about you." Mr. Sutcliffe's eyes grew glassy and his face flushed red with anger. "You truly are a very, very clever girl, aren't you?"

Ginger took a step back, very conscious that he stood between her and the doorway out of the flat and held a weapon in his hand.

"Why couldn't you have just let it be? It would have been so much better if you had just… given… up!"

"It was all for show, wasn't it?" Ginger said, backing away with two more small steps. "You employed me just to distract the officials. The dramatic way you left the match was pure theatrics. You bet against your own team, in order to make the money you needed to pay your debtors."

"Shut up!"

"No one would suspect that you fixed the match, not if your lucky bat had been stolen. No one would ever guess that you'd let your team, your friends, lose just so you could win a bet. Especially if you had employed a detective."

Neville Sutcliffe took a step towards her, raising the bat while continuing to shake his head from side to side.

"Why did you have to do this? Why are you making me do this?"

Ginger was fully aware that he was at least a foot taller than her and had considerable reach and a powerful swing. She took two more steps back. "You leaked the story to the press, didn't you? You wanted them all to see that the team's loss wasn't really your fault."

"It was just temporary." His voice caught, and he wiped at his watering eyes. "I would have produced the bat in another match or two, proclaiming it found again after I had chased down an imaginary thief. It would have worked!"

Ginger backed away a few more steps. She needed to create some distance. Mr. Sutcliffe lifted the bat, holding the handle with his left hand while resting the toe of it on his right hand, tapping it up and down on his palm. A myriad of conflicting emotions could be read on his face. He took one more step.

"You don't want to kill me, Mr. Sutcliffe."

"You're right. I don't. But I have to. I'm so sorry."

Ginger reached into her handbag, keeping her eyes fixed on his. "My first husband, Daniel, gave me a gift just before the war." Her fingers gripped a comforting cold, metallic shape. She pulled it out and pointed. Mr. Sutcliffe stopped in his tracks. "Cute little thing, isn't it? An American Remington Derringer model 95, actually,"

She paused for effect as he blinked back tears.

"I can assure you, Mr. Sutcliffe, that it is fully loaded, and I am a superb marksman." Ginger kept her voice sharp and steady as she aimed the barrel directly between her mark's eyes. "I don't like being toyed with, Mr. Sutcliffe."

"My career is over." His shoulders slumped as the bat hit the floor. "My reputation is ruined."

Ginger lowered her pistol. For a moment she almost felt sorry for the man, but at the same time she was also very angry at being deceived. "Reputation can be like a pendulum," she said, echoing her own words from a few days ago. "Sometimes it swings the wrong way."

8

———

"This is all very disappointing," Basil said as he sipped his coffee over breakfast the next morning. Mrs. Beasley had put out a very nice breakfast of bacon, eggs, toast and jam, and kippers. Ginger fed a piece of bacon to Boss, who sat expectantly on his hind legs.

"Middlesex has lost its star player, and I have suddenly no reason to attend any matches anytime soon."

"Well, that's a pity, Basil," Ginger said with empathy, "but I'm sure they will recover. Perhaps it will be a chance for other players on the team to come to the fore."

"Yes, I suppose so. That young Mr. Ashton shows a lot of promise as an all-rounder. I'll have to keep an eye on the sports section of the press to see what he will do."

Ginger hummed, trying to keep the disinterest out of her voice. She wouldn't mind if she didn't go to another cricket match for a while, and she had no interest in reading the sports section of the press.

"How are you feeling, love?" Basil refilled her coffee cup. "I know you had a rough time with this one, being lied to outright by your client."

"Yes, and what irritates me the most is that I didn't see it coming." Ginger tapped her greasy lips with her linen napkin. "I mean, I did have reservations, and I did feel something wasn't quite right even from the beginning when we first encountered Mr. Sutcliffe at Lord's, but I just couldn't put my finger on it."

"Don't be too hard on yourself. The case was solved after all. You uncovered a great lie, and you brought the questionable practice of sports betting to the public eye again. You did a good thing. Not to mention you helped solve an international art theft crime we have been working on for months!"

Ginger kissed Basil on the cheek. "Thank you, love. Of course you're right. I'm just a bit cross with myself for allowing myself to be fooled."

Boss pawed Ginger's thigh. "This is the last piece!"

"You spoil him."

"I know I do. But look at that face!"

Basil and Ginger stared at Boss who seemed to smile back, his pink, wet tongue hanging freely. Basil appeared unimpressed. Ginger turned the subject back to their case.

"Is Mr. Sutcliffe going to jail?"

"It depends on the Middlesex organisation, and if it decides to press charges. You could also press charges if you were inclined, you know. He lied to you and employed you on false pretences. The word *fraud* comes to mind, not to mention how he threatened your life." Basil frowned. "Perhaps, *I'll* press charges!"

Ginger shook her head. "I have no interest in ever thinking about Mr. Sutcliffe or the sport again."

"Mr. Sutcliffe I understand, but cricket?"

Ginger raised a red brow.

"Well, that's a shame but I do understand. Polo perhaps?"

"People on a field chasing after balls and hitting them with their silly bats?" Ginger chuckled. "Sounds too familiar. No thanks."

"Those are called mallets, love. How about rugby?"

Ginger waved her manicured hand dismissively. "Too brutal."

"Hockey?"

Ginger stared back, disbelieving.

"Right, no sticks either," Basil said. "There's fencing."

She rolled her eyes.

"Tennis?" he asked hopefully.

"Superstitious players and their lucky racquets everywhere," Ginger replied. "No thank you."

"Boxing?"

Ginger scrunched her nose as if recoiling from an offensive odour.

"Rowing?"

"Too much yelling."

"Chess then!" Basil said triumphantly.

"Boring."

"I'm running out of ideas."

"I was thinking about something slightly more sophisticated." She felt a small smile tug at the corner of her mouth.

"More sophisticated than chess?" Basil said. "Like what?"

"I hear there's the shin-kicking championships over in the Cotswolds."

Boss lifted his head to the sound of Basil struggling not to choke on his coffee.

———

MURDER ON EATON SQUARE
The Ginger Gold Mysteries Book # 10

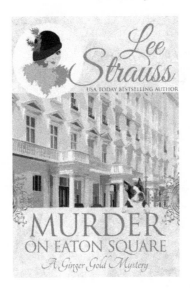

Murder's Bad Karma. . .

Life couldn't be better on Eaton Square Gardens where the most prestigious families lived, until one of their own dies and it's *murder*.

Ginger and Basil are on the case, but it's not a simple glass of bubbly fizz. The more the clues present themselves, the trickier the puzzle gets, and Ginger feels she's on a wild goose chase.

But as someone close to the victim so aptly quips, "One shouldn't commit murder. It's bad karma."

Reaping what one sows is hardly a great cup of tea.

On Amazon!

Did you know that Ginger kept a Journal?

Sign up for Lee's newsletter to get access to this exclusive content. Find out about Ginger's Life before the SS *Rosa* and how she became the woman she has. This is a fluid document that will cover her romance with her late husband Daniel, her time serving in the British secret service during World War One, and beyond. Includes a recipe for Dark Dutch Chocolate Cake!

Read on to learn more!

GINGER GOLD'S JOURNAL

Sign up for Lee's readers list and gain access to **Ginger Gold's private Journal.** Find out about Ginger's Life before the SS *Rosa* and how she became the woman she has. This is a fluid document that will cover her romance with her late husband Daniel, her time serving in the British secret service during World War One, and beyond. Includes a recipe for Dark Dutch Chocolate Cake!

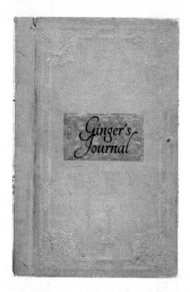

It begins: **July 31, 1912**

How fabulous that I found this Journal today, hidden in the bottom of my wardrobe. Good old Pippins, our English butler in London, gave it to me as a parting gift when Father whisked me away on our American adventure so he could marry Sally. Pips said it was for me to record my new adventures. I'm ashamed I never even penned one word before today. I think I was just too sad.

This old leather-bound journal takes me back to that emotional time. I had shed enough tears to fill the ocean and I remember telling Father dramatically that I was certain to cause flooding to match God's. At eight years old I was well-trained in my biblical studies, though, in retro-spect, I would say that I had probably bordered on heresy with my little tantrum.

The first week of my "adventure" was spent with a tummy ache and a number of embarrassing sessions that involved a bucket and Father holding back my long hair so I wouldn't soil it with vomit.

I certainly felt that I was being punished for some reason. Hartigan House—though large and sometimes lonely—was my home and Pips was my good friend. He often helped me to pass the time with games of I Spy and Xs and Os.

"Very good, Little Miss," he'd say with a twinkle in his blue eyes when I won, which I did often. I suspect now that our good butler wasn't beyond letting me win even when unmerited.

Father had got it into his silly head that I needed a mother, but I think the truth was he wanted a wife. Sally, a woman half my father's age, turned out to be a sufficient wife in the end, but I could never claim her as a mother.

Well, Pips, I'm sure you'd be happy to know that things turned out all right here in America.

SUBSCRIBE to read more!

.

ABOUT THE AUTHORS

Lee Strauss is the bestselling author of The Ginger Gold Mysteries series, The Higgins & Hawke Mystery series (cozy historical mysteries), A Nursery Rhyme Mystery series (mystery suspense), The Perception series (young adult dystopian), The Light & Love series (sweet romance), and young adult historical fiction with over a million books read. She has titles published in German, Spanish and Korean, and a growing audio library.

Norm Strauss is a singer-songwriter and performing artist who's seen the stage of The Voice of Germany. Short story writing is a new passion he shares with his wife Lee Strauss.

For more info on books by Lee Strauss and her social media links, visit leestraussbooks.com. To make sure you don't miss the next new release, be sure to sign up for her readers' list!

Did you know you can follow your favourite authors on Bookbub? If you subscribe to Bookbub — (and if you don't, why don't you? - They'll send you daily emails alerting you to sales and new releases on just the kind of books you like to read!) — follow me to make sure you don't miss the next Ginger Gold Mystery!

follow me on
goodreads

www.leestraussbooks.com
leestraussbooks@gmail.com

BOOKS BY LEE STRAUSS

On AMAZON

Ginger Gold Mysteries (cozy 1920s historical)

Cozy. Charming. Filled with Bright Young Things. This Jazz Age murder mystery will entertain and delight you with its 1920s flair and pizzazz!

Murder on the SS *Rosa*

Murder at Hartigan House

Murder at Bray Manor

Murder at Feathers & Flair

Murder at the Mortuary

Murder at Kensington Gardens

Murder at St. Georges Church

Murder Aboard the Flying Scotsman

Murder at the Boat Club

Murder on Eaton Square

Murder by Plum Pudding

Murder on Fleet Street

Murder at Brighton Beach

Lady Gold Investigates (Ginger Gold companion short stories)

Volume 1

Volume 2

Volume 3

Higgins & Hawke Mysteries (cozy 1930s historical)

The 1930s meets Rizzoli & Isles in this friendship depression era cozy mystery series.

Death at the Tavern

Death on the Tower

Death on Hanover

A Nursery Rhyme Mystery (mystery/sci fi)

Marlow finds himself teamed up with intelligent and savvy Sage Farrell, a girl so far out of his league he feels blinded in her presence - literally - damned glasses! Together they work to find the identity of @gingerbreadman. Can they stop the killer before he strikes again?

Gingerbread Man

Life Is but a Dream

Hickory Dickory Dock

Twinkle Little Star

The Perception Trilogy (YA dystopian mystery)

Zoe Vanderveen is a GAP—a genetically altered person. She lives in the security of a walled city on prime water-front property along side other equally beautiful people with extended life spans. Her brother Liam is missing. Noah Brody, a boy on the outside, is the only one who can help ~ but can she trust him?

Perception

Volition

Contrition

Light & Love (sweet romance)

Set in the dazzling charm of Europe, follow Katja, Gabriella, Eva, Anna and Belle as they find strength, hope and love.

Sing me a Love Song

Your Love is Sweet

In Light of Us

Lying in Starlight

Playing with Matches (WW2 history/romance)

A sobering but hopeful journey about how one young Germany boy copes with the war and propaganda. Based on true events.

As Elle Lee Strauss

The Clockwise Collection (YA time travel romance)

Casey Donovan has issues: hair, height and uncontrollable trips to the 19th century! And now this ~ she's accidentally taken Nate Mackenzie, the cutest boy in the school, back in time. Awkward.

Clockwise

Clockwiser

Like Clockwork

Counter Clockwise

Clockwork Crazy

<u>Standalones</u>

Seaweed

Love, Tink

ACKNOWLEDGMENTS

A special thanks to Bob Oldfield and Jeff Grady for invaluable help with all those confusing cricket terms.

As always, big shout outs to Angelika Offenwanger and Heather Belleguelle for their editing finesse!

9 781774 090725